"Three months," Nico said.

"Then we go back to business as usual. Until then, you are mine and I am yours. Better learn how to act like it."

Athena hiked up her chin. "Can *you* act like it?"

His fingers trailed down her cheek and he rubbed a thumb over her bottom lip. The caress wasn't gentle; it bordered on rough and she loved the eroticism of it.

"Can I act like I want you? Like my hands itch to get tangled in these beautiful curls? Or that my body is on the verge of taking you down to this floor and covering you like the animal you think I am?"

He slipped the tip of his thumb between her lips. Her tongue barely dabbed the skin before he withdrew.

Nico stepped back. She blinked against the abrupt return to reality.

"I think I have it covered," he said, arching a dark eyebrow.

* * *

Black Sheep Bargain by Naima Simone
is part of the Billionaires of Boston series.

Dear Reader,

Coming to the end of a series is always a mixed bag of emotion. I'm happy and excited because, yes! Everyone will finally have their happily-ever-after. But I'm also sad because it's truly over. I won't be visiting this world and characters I've spent the last couple of years with. I'm bidding it farewell. Nope, that was *not* a tear!

When I first imagined the Farrell brothers, I knew there would be four of them, even though only three were mentioned in Barron's will. There's something mysterious, alluring and sexy about the black sheep, and he's always been one of my favorite hero types. So I knew the fourth brother had to be the unknown, rejected black sheep of the family. And then throw in revenge fueled by love of family? That's a hero after my own heart! And Nico Morgan just tugged on all of my heartstrings even though his outer shell is tough. But Athena Evans is no pushover. She's more than his match, and writing their rocky but emotional and sensual road to love was so much fun.

I hope you enjoy this final chapter of the Billionaires of Boston world and fall in love with Nico and Athena!

Happy reading!

Naima

NAIMA SIMONE

—

BLACK SHEEP BARGAIN

HARLEQUIN
DESIRE

HARLEQUIN®
DESIRE™

Recycling programs
for this product may
not exist in your area.

ISBN-13: 978-1-335-58136-5

Black Sheep Bargain

Copyright © 2022 by Naima Simone

For questions and comments about the quality of this book, please contact us at CustomerService@Harlequin.com.

Harlequin Enterprises ULC
22 Adelaide St. West, 41st Floor
Toronto, Ontario M5H 4E3, Canada
www.Harlequin.com

Printed in U.S.A.

USA TODAY bestselling author **Naima Simone**'s love of romance was first stirred by Harlequin books pilfered from her grandmother. Now she spends her days writing sizzling romances with a touch of humor and snark.

She is wife to her own real-life superhero and mother to two awesome kids. They live in perfect domestically challenged bliss in the southern United States.

Books by Naima Simone

Harlequin Desire

Billionaires of Boston

Vows in Name Only
Secrets of a One Night Stand
The Perfect Fake Date
Black Sheep Bargain

HQN Books

The Road to Rose Bend
Christmas in Rose Bend
With Love from Rose Bend

Visit her Author Profile page
at Harlequin.com for more titles.

You can also find Naima Simone on Facebook,
along with other Harlequin Desire authors, at
Facebook.com/HarlequinDesireAuthors!

One

Whoever said "revenge is a dish best served cold" clearly possessed a lack of imagination.

When not administered immediately, the other person might forget they had it coming. Or they might have one of those "come to Jesus" moments where they're not the same bastard who deserved their comeuppance.

Or worse.

The person might die.

Oh no. Revenge was definitely a dish served piping hot and shoved down the throat.

Nico Morgan stood on the sidewalk outside the Brighton bakery on Washington Street, traffic a cacophony of horns and squeals. Pedestrians flowed around him, separating like the tide, caught up in heading to work, classes or the local coffee shops.

But none of the other bakeries in this neighborhood

could compare to the baked goods tucked in the glass cases of Evans Bakery.

The name was as simple as the food and family inside.

Well...most of the family.

Giving the brick building with the pristine white, green and yellow awning one last glance, he strode forward and opened the wide door. There was a painting of an elegant white cake and chocolate chip cookies on the sparkling glass. If his memory was correct—and his memory was always correct, since he never forgot a medication dose, a profit or loss, or a slight—Glory Evans ensured her staff cleaned this glass every morning without fail. And a couple times through the day if needed. The older woman's motto had been, Dirty Windows, Dirty Ovens. His private investigator's report had noted Glory's death earlier this year, after she never fully recovered from her stroke a few years ago. And her granddaughter had now assumed responsibility of day-to-day operations.

As he stepped inside, the scents of sugar, vanilla, baked bread and freshly brewed coffee greeted him. Most people would find it odd that the sweet and nutty aromas had lust pumping through his veins. But then most people wouldn't take one look at the woman pushing through the swinging kitchen door and associate those scents with her.

Athena Evans.

Nico clenched his jaw, narrowing his eyes on the slender yet sensually curved manager of the bakery as she warmly greeted customers, holding conversations even though her slim arms bore the burden of a wide silver tray loaded with pastries. He tracked her slow but steady progress through the crowded space, tracing the familiar lines of her face, the delicate set of her shoulders, the seductive yet somehow innocent sway of her hips, the stride of those long, toned legs.

There wasn't a damn thing innocent about Athena Evans.

He had personal and intimate knowledge of that.

Athena called out to the shorter woman behind the counter—her sister. Returning his scrutiny to her face, he caught the subtle uptick of warmth in her smile— hell, in her entire expression. That's because Athena didn't just smile with her mouth. Never had. It began there with a shockingly sexual curve, but it also softened the sharpness of her cheekbones, brightened her hazel eyes so they appeared more green than golden brown. It loosened her shoulders, relaxed the straight line of her spine.

It'd been one of the most beautiful things about her.

It'd also come to be one of the things he resented most about her.

Today, her sister was the recipient of that show of affection as Athena rounded the corner of the bakery case, tray held high, arms not showing the slightest sign of strain. His breath stuttered in his chest at that negligent display of strength. Desire pulsed in his veins as he studied the flex of sleek muscle revealed by the sleeveless yellow sundress that emphasized the beauty of her dark brown skin. With an ease that would've shamed an award-winning body builder, she set the tray on top of the case, not appearing winded or tired. Years toiling in the family bakery would build up that kind of stamina.

Besides, even if Athena were bone weary, she would never let on. That's not what the perfect daughter, granddaughter or sister did.

And Nico counted on that futile pursuit of perfection to aid him in his own endgame.

It was the only reason he stood in his ex-lover's place of employment three years after she ended their relationship, willing to face her "fuck you, now get the hell out."

Oh, the things one was willing to do to for revenge. Anything.

Anticipation swirled in his chest. Yes, because all the plans he'd worked on, *existed for* were slowly coming to fruition. But also because he stood in *this* shop, within feet of *this* woman. Electric currents raced over his skin. Waiting for her to notice him. To look at him so he could glimpse the shock, the hate, the... He was a succubus, greedy for any emotion, any reaction.

Three years.

Three years he'd gone without allowing himself even the sight of her. But now, with an unforeseen twist of fate, he needed her. No one else but Athena Evans would do. And he could indulge himself in her.

Until their business was done.

Then *he* would be the one to end it. To walk away.

Because three years ago, Athena had reminded him of a very important lesson. Never become attached.

Only trust the one person who will never let you down—yourself.

Athena removed the eclairs and doughnuts from the tray, talking to her sister and the customers at the counter. As she finished up, she scanned the lobby, and he braced himself. Objectively, he should've been wary of the trickle of eagerness that invaded him. But he ignored it, chalking it up to excitement over the imminent commencement of his plans. Not to the moment when she...

Her eyes locked with his. They widened.

Filled with shock, horror—and fury.

He smiled.

Without removing her gaze from his, she leaned down and said something in her sister's ear. Whatever it was had Geneva Evans's head jerking his way with a glare. His smile didn't falter. Satisfaction burned so fucking bright inside him, it rivaled the iconic streetlamps outside his Beacon Hill home. Geneva nodded, and Athena emerged from behind the bakery cases and forged a straight path to him. This time, she didn't pause to hold pleasant conversations with customers. No, she marched toward him, that affable smile nowhere in sight.

And when she stopped in front of him, smelling of sugar, butter and freshly baked bread, the cold glitter in her hazel eyes didn't stop him from hungering to sink his teeth into that place where throat and shoulder met...and take a bite.

"What the hell are you doing here?" Then before he could answer, she gave her head a shake. "You know what? Don't answer that. Because I don't give a damn. Just leave."

He arched an eyebrow. "You don't want me to do that."

"Oh, I assure you, I really do."

"I need to speak with you, Athena. Five minutes.

What's five minutes compared to three years?" he asked, pausing as her lips twisted down at the corners. Anger slashed through his chest, but he smothered it. Maybe at one time he'd given a fuck that she'd walked out on him, but not now. He'd have to care about her to feel anything about it. "Trust me. You want to hear what I have to say."

"Trust you." She crossed her arms over her chest. "Those are words you might not want to lead with," she muttered.

"Sticks and stones, and all that, Athena," he murmured. "Or should I say, pot meet kettle?" He cocked his head. "We can stand here and trade compliments or you can follow me outside so we can talk, and then you can get back to your duties in the kitchen."

He smiled, and it didn't feel pretty. Probably because it wasn't. When they'd been together, she'd enjoyed playing the role of Cinderella for her family, so he'd call it like he saw it.

"Still an asshole, I see."

She returned his smile. It differed so much from the one she'd given her sister that he would've laughed if he didn't know that would antagonize her further. Her earlier smile had contained love, warmth. This one was nothing more than a baring of teeth. Good. He didn't need her affection for this. Preferred her animosity. At least then he knew where they stood.

At least then there was a little bit of honesty between them.

"Still choosing a life of martyrdom and blind devotion, I see," he said smoothly, with only a tiny hint of bite. After all, it was her sense of sacrifice that would work in his favor. For once. He sighed, glancing down at his antique gold Omega Speedmaster Moonwatch. "Five minutes, and then I'm leaving. And, Athena..." He leaned down so their faces were inches apart. So he could pick out the golden striations in her green and brown eyes. "You'll regret it if I do."

Anger flared in her gaze, but so did uncertainty. Most likely because during the year and a half they'd been together, she'd never known him to exaggerate or threaten. He didn't need to.

No, he promised. Then followed through.

"Five minutes." She jerked her chin toward the back of the store. "In my office, not outside."

Not permitting him a moment to disagree, she pivoted on her wedge heel and strode across the store. At a more measured pace, he followed, aware of the curious stares shadowing them. But all of his attention was focused on the woman in front of him. On the gorgeous halo of dark brown curls that grazed her tense shoulders. On the slender back that flared into rounded hips and the ass that deserved its own religion.

He jerked his gaze away. She—and her ass—no longer had the power to influence him. Yes, Athena was a gorgeous woman; he would be a liar to deny that. But he'd allowed that beauty to lead him around by his dick one time before. Never again.

Athena pushed through the wide, swinging door that led into the kitchen and veered to the left, toward a brightly lit hallway. Framed photos decorated the walls here, as they did in the bakery's main room. Black-and-white pictures of the shop from the 1960s when it first opened as well as color images of the present day. Pictures of the family over decades, showcasing a shift in fashion and generations. The display proudly declared a heritage, a legacy along with a family business.

And he knew from their many conversations, Athena was determined to carry that tradition forward into the future. At any cost.

Pausing before a closed door, she slipped a key ring out of her dress pocket. She unlocked the office and entered, leaving the door open in silent invitation. Accepting it, he moved inside the small room that contained her scent and her stamp. Potted plants in the windowsills. More framed pictures of family on the desk. Cookbooks and tin boxes that looked familiar because they used to take up space on his bookshelves.

Opting to stand instead of taking a chance with the folding chair in front of her desk, he crossed his arms and met her steady gaze. She, too, stood behind the ancient, scratched desk.

"I'm sure you didn't travel all the way over to Brighton to stare at me since you could've done that anytime in the last three years. So what is this mysterious important topic you need to see me about?" she asked with no small amount of sarcasm.

"Barron died."

Her low gasp echoed in the room, and for just a second, sympathy softened her features, thawed the chips of ice in her eyes. Anger flickered in him like a struck flame, dancing to an unseen wind. She could keep her pity. He had no need of it.

And Barron sure as hell didn't deserve it.

"I'm sorry, Nico," she murmured.

A shiver stumbled down his spine, and only by sheer

will did he not reveal his reaction to his name wrapped around her tongue. That same tongue might as well have been hugging his dick, that's how eroticly the sound had struck him.

And it seemed sacrilegious that the first time she'd spoken his name in three years was to apologize for the death of the man who'd donated sperm to his mother over thirty years ago.

Fuck her compassion.

"I'm not," he stated, blunt, hard.

She stared at him, and he met her gaze without flinching.

"How long?"

"Almost nine months."

"Really?" She frowned. "I hadn't heard. Not that I follow news from the corporate business world but…" She shook her head. "Still that's big. Are you…okay?"

"Am I okay?" He smiled. "Oh, Athena, I'm ecstatic. The bastard is roasting in hell. It doesn't get much better than that."

If only his mother had lived to see it—that would've made Barron Farrell's death sweeter.

After all the years of pain and suffering Rhoda Morgan had been through after he'd abandoned her with an infant, she should've stood by that graveside. It'd been her right, her due.

"Is that what you came here to tell me?" she asked, confusion coloring her voice. "That Barron Farrell is gone? Because while I hate to sound insensi—"

He waved a hand through the air in front of him. "No, I wouldn't walk across a room to talk about Barron's death, much less drive the twenty minutes from downtown to deliver the news. And while a part of me finds a great deal of satisfaction in him attaining his great reward, I'm also upset about it."

"That's understandable." She nodded, and a gentle note threaded through her voice. "Your feelings toward him must be...complicated. There must have been things you wanted to say to him before he—"

Nico's harsh bark of laughter interrupted her. "Complicated? My feelings for Barron Farrell were the simplest of all human emotions. Hate. Utter contempt. But you're right. There were things I wanted to tell him before he died. Like what a heartless bastard he was. Like that he didn't deserve to be called a 'man,' much less a father. And that one day he would know how it felt to have his world stripped of everything he loved. And I would be there to witness it. I would be the one to watch it all crumble around him."

"But he stole that from you. By dying."

Anger, scalding hot and brutal, slammed into him. "Yes," he snapped. "He robbed me of my right to pay him back for every tear my mother cried, every dime she scraped together, every prematurely gray hair she grew."

Fuck.

This wasn't how he'd planned this discussion. Shoving his hands into his front pants pockets, he paced across the office, attempting to expend the agitation crawling through him. But the tiny room didn't offer enough space, and he pivoted, retracing his steps until he stared at a battered gray file cabinet and a potted plant with overflowing leaves. Another framed photo sat on top. This one of Athena and Glory Evans outside the bakery.

Family.

How she clung to them like a buoy in a wind-tossed lake.

With his mother gone, he didn't have those moorings.

She'd been gone a year now, and God, did he miss her. In the worst of those moments—like early Sunday mornings when he didn't have her apartment to visit for breakfast before their weekly visits to Faneuil Hall Marketplace and SoWa Vintage Market—he convinced himself he was better off without those ties. No ties meant no waiting for them to be cut. No depending on people who could walk without a moment's notice or explanation.

No dying and leaving you broken and alone.

No using those same ties like a web to tangle and trap.

As he intended to do with Athena.

Guilt flickered in his chest but he smothered it. That didn't belong here. Not with her. And not when it came to Barron. Neither one of them had looked back when they'd left him. He hadn't been enough for either of them. So no, he didn't harbor any regret or shame for his course of action.

This was for him.

And for his mother.

"He's gone, Nico. You can't exact revenge on a dead man," she said in that same soft tone. The tone that reminded him of a time when he'd shared parts of himself with her that he'd hidden from everyone else except his

mother. Reminded him of a time when he'd believed…
in her. In them.

When he'd believed in a lie.

"That's where you're wrong."

He turned from his contemplation of the picture and
faced her again. Maybe she sensed something in his
voice, his demeanor. Or maybe, even after three years,
she still knew him. A fine tension entered her frame,
stiffening her shoulders.

"What're you talking about?"

"It means, he might be dead but his legacy is very
much alive. Farrell International still continues to oper-
ate, and under his sons, thrive. If he's beyond my reach,
I'll go after the only thing he's ever cared about—that
company."

"Wait, wait." She held up her hands. "Sons? I thought
you said he only had one son, aside from you."

"No, apparently Barron made a habit of fathering
children, then abandoning them and their mothers,"
he said. "The news hit all the business papers and gossip sites. At the reading of Barron Farrell's will, Cain
Farrell discovered not only that he had two, unknown
younger brothers, but that he also had to share his in-
heritance with them. Farrell International. Barron had
a stipulation that they all must work together at the
company for one year or else Farrell would be disman-
tled and sold. They chose to stay, and in the last nine
months, the business has done very well. Possibly better than it did under Barron's control."

She shook her head, frowning and winding a finger
in the air. "Back it up a minute. You said Cain Farrell
discovered he had *two* brothers. That's wrong. Unless

you're one of the two?" Then she waved her hands, frowning. "No, that can't be right," she said, answering her own question. "Because you're not working for Farrell International."

"It's not wrong. Barron included the illegitimate sons he meant to acknowledge in his will. And continued to deny the existence of the one he'd been denying for over thirty years," he drawled.

Her full mouth flattened into a grim line, and her hazel eyes narrowed with a gleam of anger.

Shock ricocheted through him. She was angry. On his behalf. Rarely did anything surprise him. But she'd just accomplished the impossible.

"I hate to speak badly of the dead but… What. An. Asshole."

The corner of his mouth twitched, but he smothered the spurt of humor. Finding Athena Evans adorable heralded a slippery slope to destruction. And since he needed her, remembering the wreckage she could leave behind—*had* left behind—was imperative. If she agreed to this—and he had no doubt she would—he'd never be so foolish as to allow her close again.

"Not that I'm unsympathetic, but I still don't understand what this has to do with me."

He approached the desk, cocked his head and studied her for a long moment. "Because you're going to help me get what I desire most, Athena. Justice."

For his mother. For himself.

She blinked. "I'm going to…help you," she slowly repeated. "I don't understand."

"I meant what I said about dismantling Barron's legacy. Stock by stock. Right now Cain and Achilles Farrell and Kenan Rhodes own the majority of shares with the remaining numbers distributed among Farrell International shareholders. Or so they believe. I've been working for years, trading and buying stocks, and I almost own just as many shares as they do. In another few weeks, I'll own more, and I'll have controlling interest in Barron's company."

"And what do you plan to do with the control, if you get it?" she asked, her gaze roaming his face as if she could find answers there.

"*When* I get it. I plan on being Barron Farrell's son." His lips lifted in a small smile.

She could take that however she wanted.

"I don't trust that purposefully enigmatic statement at all." She scoffed, crossing her arms. "But it doesn't matter because I want no part of—" she flicked her fingers "—whatever this is."

"Oh but you're not just 'a part,' Athena, you're going to be my partner."

Her chin snapped back, shock flaring in her eyes. Slowly, her arms dropped to her sides and she stared at him. Tension crackled in the room, popping over his skin, even through his suit jacket and shirt. Exhilaration. It sang in his veins.

How could he have forgotten that she'd never had a problem challenging him, going head-to-head with him? Where others showed him deference and even fear, she'd dared him with her gaze, her words…her body. No, Athena Evans had never kneeled before him.

Unless she desired to be there.

"And why the hell would I do that when being your partner the first time was so overrated?" Her mouth twisted into something not quite a sneer. "No, I think I'll pass. But hey, thanks for stopping by. Don't let another three years go by. Or I don't know…do."

"Do you know what your brother has been up to, Athena?" he asked, flattening his palms on the desktop and leaning forward. "While you've been chained to this bakery, undoubtedly running yourself ragged to keep the lights on and the employees paid, do you have any idea what your brother has been doing behind your back?"

If he hadn't been scrutinizing her so closely, he might've missed the glimmer of anxiety in her gaze. But he did spot it. He also noted that nothing else about her expression or demeanor changed.

Still the Evans family gatekeeper. The fierce protector.

He counted on that fierce loyalty.

And yet an ember of anger sparked to life deep in his chest. That same blind devotion to people who, yes, loved her, but who had never appreciated her or offered her the same consideration she showed them—that's what had broken her and Nico. She'd walked away, never looking back.

Today, she had no choice but to look back. He'd made sure of that.

He reached inside his jacket and removed three folded sheets of paper. Without breaking their visual connection, he set the thin sheaf on the desk and slid it across to her. After a long moment, she lowered her gaze and stared at the paper as if scared to touch it.

Smart.

Because she knew Randall Evans. Knew what he was capable of.

Nico could call Athena a number of things, and in those days after she left him, he had, but none of those names had included *coward*. And she reinforced that opinion when her jaw firmed and she picked up the stack, unfolded it and read the top paper. She wouldn't need to read the rest. The first page with Promissory Note boldly printed across the top would declare its purpose.

Straightening, he waited while she scanned the note, already knowing what she read. A three-hundred-thousand-dollar loan Randall Evans took out with a local bank, putting up the bakery as collateral. Which he could do since, as the oldest child, the shop had gone to him when Glory Evans had died earlier that year.

Correction.

Oldest *biological* child.

Technically Athena was the oldest child, but she was also adopted. And apparently not good enough to inherit the Evans's precious bakery.

And yet even after that slight, Athena still stayed.

That ember inside him flared into a flame.

"This can't be…" she whispered.

"True? Real?" He arched an eyebrow. "Why? Because he's above this? Because he wouldn't do this without talking to you first? Because he wouldn't put your business in debt when you're already struggling to pay bills, to make payroll, to stay afloat?"

She glanced away from him and that's all the answer he needed.

She looked down at the note again, her fingers fisting the paper. "It states here that the maturity date isn't for another two years. Why are you showing me this now?"

"The loan would be due in two years if your brother were making the monthly payments. As of today, he's six months behind, and the bank is about to proceed with calling the loan. If that happens... No, *when* that happens—the entire balance will be due, and if your brother cannot pay it, they will take their collateral."

Her eyes closed, her lips moving on a silent curse. The note in her hand shook before she deliberately set it on the desktop. Spinning on her heel, she thrust her fingers through her hair, striding away from the paper as if being anywhere in its vicinity offended her— threatened her.

Yes, that was more accurate. Because that had been real fear Nico had glimpsed in her eyes before she'd shut them. His fingers and palm tingled with the need to... What? Tear that loan from the desk and shred it to pieces? Wouldn't change the fact that her brother had screwed her and the family by being the same selfish, self-absorbed ass he'd always been.

To cup her shoulders, turn her around and press her to his chest? To hold her?

No, that was no longer his right. And even if she'd allow it, he wouldn't. One touch to silken skin, one in- halation of her warm, sweet scent and he'd trick himself into believing maybe he could trust her. That she'd stick.

Only one person in his life had ever stuck. And she was gone.

All he had was himself.

And the certainty that Athena was devoted to an un- grateful, spoiled family.

Athena stopped in front of the small window that offered an uninspiring view of the back lot. The silence in the office stretched, but Nico didn't break it. Unlike most people, especially in the social circles he now swam in, he didn't mind the quiet. When a person grew up in Roxbury, where peace and silence were rare commodities, one valued the moments void of noise and confusion.

But nothing about the quiet in this office was peaceful or calm. He didn't need to see her face to feel the turmoil that emanated from her. The bend of her head, exposing the vulnerable nape of her neck, the slight slump of her shoulders and the flutter of her lashes against her striking cheekbones all relayed a story.

Weariness.

Worry.

Defeat.

Something ugly slashed through him. He'd caused that.

She should never wear that. It didn't fit.

Fuck.

He took an involuntary step toward her—

"What is making that disappear going to cost me?" She pivoted, facing him again.

That unruffled, cool mask firmly back in place. Relief cascaded through him. *Good.* He didn't want a crushed Athena. He needed the warrior she was named after. And this woman, staring at him with contempt in her eyes, didn't tempt him to do something as foolish as reconsider his path. Or her part in it.

"That's why you're here, right?" she continued. "That's the offer I would regret not hearing? You need me to—how did you put it?—be your partner, or what? You allow the bank to call the loan?"

"Yes." Her sharp inhalation blew on the flame of anger still dancing in his chest. "That's your and your parents' job, to clean up after your brother's messes, not mine. You agree to the terms of my bargain and I'll pay off the loan. Evans Bakery will be debt free and safe. Until the next time. And we both know there will be a next time."

"What are these terms?" she ground out.

He slid his hands in his pockets again. So he would resist touching her, trying to shake some sense into her about the futility of covering for a nearly thirty-year-old man who persisted in behaving like a boy. Nico could see why her parents did. But her? No, he'd never get it.

"You pretend to be my fiancée for the next three months. That includes attending social and business events, dinners, parties or wherever I deem your presence necessary. Your job as my fiancée is to convince everyone, especially Cain and Achilles Farrell and Kenan Rhodes, as well as their significant others, that we are in love, devoted to one another and a solid couple. In other words, Athena, your sole purpose is to make me look like a good guy."

"I am not a goddamn genie," she snapped. "Because that's what you need to pull that off." Loosing a disbelieving laugh, she dropped her head back and pinched the bridge of her nose. "What the hell?" she muttered softly before raising her head and spearing him with a narrowed glare. "Do you hear how crazy this sounds? I mean, seriously. Play it back in your head and give it a minute. Maybe the absurdity of it hasn't had time to sink in." She shook her head. "Of all the things I expected you to say when you popped up in here this morning, Nico, that didn't even climb into the top twenty."

"And yet, you're going to agree. Because if you do, you'll keep this bakery. If you don't, you'll lose it. Those are your choices."

"Why?" she asked, the question bursting from her. Her desperation unmistakable. "Why me? And what is this…charade supposed to gain you?" Once more, she tunneled her fingers through her hair, dragging the thick curls away from her face and offering him a clear, unrestricted view of the frustration etched on her features. "Why are you doing this?" she finally whispered.

"Why you?" he arched an eyebrow. "Expediency and practicality. I don't have the time or patience to find a woman who will play the role of a woman who knows me when I already have one who does. And so well." He paused, letting his gaze roam over those jeweled eyes, the perfect slash of cheekbones, the decadent curve of her mouth and drop down to her slender body with its wicked, lush curves. "Besides, another woman might get ideas. This is an arrangement. Nothing more. When the three months are up, I don't want to go through the trouble of breaking off something that was never real to begin with. You, I have no worries, will have no problem leaving."

She'd already shown him she was so damn good at it.

"And with you by my side, I'll gain entry into Barron's sons' tight little circle without suspicion. Who would look wrong at a happily engaged man? And by the time we show up at just about every social event where they and their wives do, I'll accomplish that goal. As for why I'm doing this?" He stepped forward, his voice lowering with the bitterness he'd hoarded for decades. "Because I can. Because that bastard will rage all the way from hell, knowing I own his beloved company. Because I can't exist in a world where the name Farrell is praised and revered when it doesn't even deserve to be spit on. It deserves to be forgotten."

She inhaled a deep breath, then slowly shook her head. "No. I won't do it. I can't do it. You're making me an accomplice to a plan to destroy lives. And if you think none of that will blow back on you, hurt you…" She held up her hands, palms out. "I can't."

"So you're saying no out of worry for my soul?" He released a harsh bark of laughter that had her flinching. The movement was infinitesimal, but he caught it. "Save your false concern. Just to be clear, you're choosing to let me leave through that door, knowing your bakery is only weeks from closing. Because if I do, I'm not coming back, Athena."

Her gaze flicked toward the note on her desk, her chest lifting and falling on another deep breath. When her eyes returned to his, the resolve there telegraphed her answer. "Yes, we're clear."

Shock rippled through him, followed by a twisted stab of emotions he hadn't experienced in three years. Fear. Doubt.

But damn if he'd let her witness them.

Dipping his head, he said, "If that's your decision," then turned and left the office without glancing back.

In the past, she had stolen his heart. Broken it. And

walked out on him. Since knowing her, she'd surprised him at every turn. Why should now be any different?

Because Athena Evans had never done the expected—even when he needed her to.

Two

Athena parked her sixteen-year-old Nissan Altima in front of her parents' Dorchester Victorian-style two-family home. As she switched the ignition off, something under the hood rattled in protest. She closed her eyes and squeezed her hands around the steering wheel.

Nico had tried to buy her a new car when they'd been together, viewing the used car as a hand-me-down from her older brother. True, it had been, but that didn't mean she valued it any less. Or needed it any less. And when her and Nico's relationship ended, she'd never been so glad she'd resisted. This was the car she'd driven away in.

"Dammit," she whispered, shaking her head. As if that could jerk loose thoughts of her ex. Of their past together. Of *them* together.

He'd reappeared after a three-year absence, hauling

open the door she'd bolted shut with heavy-duty locks. Now she couldn't shove him back in. And she'd tried. God knows she'd tried.

But one look at him standing in the bakery, and it had all rushed in like a swollen flood crashing through a flimsy dam. The dizzying exhilaration. The thrilling excitement. The blinding pain. The scalding anger.

The consuming lust.

She shivered.

Only Nico Morgan had ever elicited such a torrent of emotion from her. A woman could hate a man for that.

Fine. She was said woman.

Groaning, she exited the car and rounded the hood, pausing at the curb. The light blue, three-story home with its two porches, rounded rooms, wide picture windows and towerlike turret had always been home, even after she'd moved out six years earlier. Her parents, her brother, Randall, and his wife, Gina, and their two children still lived there. As had Mama when she'd been alive.

Pain, agonizing, scored her chest, and she lifted a fist, rubbing it over her sternum. Eight months. It'd been eight months since Mama had passed, and the grief, the ache had eased some. But it still took her aback at times. More often when she visited here, where the essence of her grandmother still lingered like the scent of the lilac powder she'd used every day after her bath. That scent, the memories—they laid into Athena every time she crossed the threshold. And today, she had to enter her childhood home from a place of strength. Especially considering the news she had to deliver.

Dragging in a breath, she held it, then slowly, deliberately let it go. And moved up the walkway toward the front porch. As if she'd been looking out the window—which was definitely a possibility since Winnie Evans loved to catch the goings-on in the neighborhood—her mother opened the door and waited for her, smiling as Athena climbed the top step.

"Hey, Mom." Athena walked across the porch and straight into her mother's outstretched arms. Hugging her tight, she closed her eyes, worry creeping through her. Was she thinner in the few days since she'd last seen her? Mama's death had hit them all hard, but her mother had barely left her bed for nearly a month afterward. "How're you feeling?"

"I'm fine, I'm fine. Stop fussing." Her mother squeezed Athena, then stepped back, cupping her upper arms. "Don't you look pretty today in your yellow? Your grandmother always loved that color on you." Patting her arm, she shifted backward, making room for Athena to enter. "Come on inside. I was surprised to get your call, but happy, too."

Guilt curdled in her belly like old milk.

If only she was just dropping by to visit and gossip. If only Nico hadn't come by the shop with his stupid bargain.

If only Randall hadn't gone behind her back and taken out *a three-hundred-thousand-dollar* loan on her bakery.

No, not her bakery. Randall's. All Randall's. And he had the documents that said so. As he'd told her many times.

Didn't matter that she rose at four every morning to make sure there were freshly baked muffins, doughnuts, cupcakes and an assortment of other pastries for their customers. Didn't matter that Randall had only showed up at the shop eleven times in the three years since Mama's stroke, not at all since she'd died—and yes, she'd kept count. Didn't matter that the staff, vendors and customers viewed her as their employer because she handled all of the managerial responsibilities.

None of it mattered because she might be the oldest child, but she wasn't blood.

An old ache bloomed behind her sternum, and she turned up the wattage on the smile for her mother to cover the hurt, to conceal the throb of rejection.

She'd become an expert at both.

"How about I fix you a cup of tea?" She looped an arm through her mother's and guided her out of the foyer. "Have you had one today?"

"Not since this morning. A cup sounds perfect, though."

They passed the gleaming oak staircase that led up to the second level and walked into the large living room with its high ceilings, round alcove and trio of floor-to-ceiling windows. The room opened off to a dining room and down another hall to the main hub of both sides of the house—Winnie's kitchen. Athena left her mother on the couch in front of the coffee table before peeling off toward the kitchen. Years had taught Athena exactly how her mother preferred her tea, and she prepared a cup, bringing it with her back into the living room ten minutes later.

"Here you go, Mom." She set it down on the coffee table, then took a seat on the couch beside her. "Are you sure everything's okay? You seem kind of…tired. Are you resting well? Eating?"

"Yes, yes and yes." Her mother softly laughed, patting her hand. "Stop worrying so much, honey. I'm fine. Now, tell me what's so important that you actually left the bakery early to come over and see me."

Right. Because she'd never leave Evans before it closed at six in the evening. Everyone in the family knew that. Randall definitely did. Just another reason he didn't bother showing up because Athena always stood in the gap to do it.

They call necessity the mother of invention for a reason. Your brother has never had to figure out how to make his own way because you and your family have always paved it for him.

Nico's voice, his admonishment from years ago, echoed in her head.

God, she needed him out of her head. Out of her life.

Why had he chosen to reenter it when she'd just started to erase him from her mind? And by *erase*, she meant go a consecutive two weeks without thoughts of him invading her sleep. Okay, a week, a week without waking up wet, trembling and aching…

Right. No dwelling on dreams of her ex while sitting next to her mother. Bad manners. And just plain awkward.

"Let me just put out there that you alone are important enough for me to leave the bakery early. You're important, period."

"Oh wow, this must be big," her mother murmured, picking up her tea and peering at Athena over the cup's rim before taking a sip.

"Mom, I mean it," Athena insisted, but then she sighed, splaying her fingers wide on her thighs. Fine, she was stalling. This was one of those Band-Aid moments—better to just rip it off and get it over with. But first... "Where's Dad? He should probably hear this, too."

"This is Tuesday so he's down at the barbershop. It'll be at another couple of hours before he's back home." Her mother frowned, setting her cup back on the table. "It's that serious? Do you want me to call him to come home? Is it one of you kids? Gina? Mya or Randall Jr.?" she pressed, naming Randal's wife and her grandchildren.

"No, Mom." Athena reached out, covering Winnie's hand and shaking her head for added emphasis. "We're all fine that I know of. This is...something else. I can tell Dad later. I just thought telling you both together would be easier." Inhaling, she straightened. *So much for ripping that bandage off.* She mentally grimaced. "I had a surprise visitor today at the bakery. Nico Morgan."

"Your ex-boyfriend?" Confusion clouded her mother's dark brown gaze and she tilted her head to the side. A second later, confusion slid into a moue of disdain. "Why did he show up? Like a bad penny. And after how long? Four years? What could he possibly want?"

"Three years," Athena corrected. But who was counting?

Winnie hadn't particularly cared for Nico. She'd believed he'd wanted to separate Athena from her family. Nico had his faults—emotionally unavailable, guarded, stubborn to a fault and too damn hot for his own good—but that one sin she couldn't lay at his feet. He hadn't sought to isolate her from her family. Set boundaries? Yes. But as someone who dearly loved his mother, he would've never demanded she cut her own from her life.

But he had put his foot down at Winnie calling at three o'clock in the morning to make sure Athena would open the bakery because her brother wasn't feeling well. Translation—he'd tied one on while hanging out with his friends the night before and was too hung over to open the store.

No, Winnie hadn't appreciated Nico sharing his thoughts on how her brother was a lazy son of a bitch who wouldn't know responsibility if it kicked him in the nuts. A direct quote.

Oh no. Winnie did not particularly care for Nico Morgan.

"Four, three," her mother said, waving a dismissive hand, "whatever. What does he want? Nothing good, I bet."

"You'd win that bet." God, how did she tell her mother this? "Mom, he showed me a banknote for a three-hundred-thousand-dollar loan that Randall took out. He used the bakery as collateral." Her mother's eyes widened, and Athena pushed ahead with the rest of it. "And he hasn't made any payments for the last six months so the bank is about to call the loan. If Randall doesn't come up with the full balance, we'll lose the bakery."

"You didn't know anything about this?"

The question shouldn't have slapped out at her. But it did. Because of the vein of accusation running through it. As if Athena were responsible for this deceitful action that could destroy the business Winnie's mother and father had defied the societal, racial and economic odds to build.

Because it was never Randall's fault.

Stop it. There's no time for this. And she didn't mean it like that. She never does.

Athena repeated the refrain to herself. Shoving the traces of bitterness down, she met her mother's gaze.

"No, I had no clue about any of it until Nico showed me a copy of the promissory note." And because she couldn't root out all the petty inside her, she added, "When you and Dad signed over control of the bakery to Randall without any kind of checks and balances, he didn't require any additional signatures or permission to apply for a loan. As a matter of fact, we don't know if this is the only one out there."

The horror slowly dawned on her. How that thought just occurred to her, she had no idea. What else had Randall been up to? And how could she find out? Could Nico—

No. Absolutely not. No way in hell she'd go to him for help.

"No, your brother wouldn't do that! Not without telling us..."

Athena stared at her mother. Only respect for the woman who had chosen to raise and love her kept the *"Are you kidding me right now?"* from exiting her mouth. But her face? Well, she couldn't control that. And Winnie was an excellent expression translator.

She threw her hands up, releasing a sound that was somewhere between a sigh and a tsk. "We don't even know if this is true. Just because it comes from Nico

Morgan, who you haven't heard from in years, we're supposed to accept it as fact? I don't believe your bro—"

"I saw the documents myself, Mom," Athena quietly, firmly interrupted. "They're real. And it's Randall's signature."

"Dear God," her mother whispered, and for the first time since Athena dropped the news, it seemed as if the gravity of her brother's actions sank in. Pressing a palm to her mouth, Winnie stared at Athena. "Three hundred thousand? Athena, what're we going to do?"

A better question would be why did Randall get the loan in the first place and what did he do with the money? He still lived with their parents. And yes, he'd recently bought new cars for him and his wife, and he always dressed to the nines, but other than that? What did he have to show for all that money?

But history had taught her that trying to nail Randall down for answers would be like attempting to nail ambrosia salad to the wall. Impossible.

"I don't know," she answered. "First thing, we need to talk to Randall. See if he has any of the money left. And if not, what were his plans to pay it back." Obviously, he didn't have any plans or he would've been making the monthly loan payments, but she left that unsaid.

"Wait, wait." Winnie held up her hands, palms out.

"Wait for what, Mom?" Athena asked, confused.

"We don't have time. *Six months*. If the bank hasn't already sent out letters demanding the balance of the loan, they soon will. We might have *weeks*, not months, before we lose the bakery."

Anger spiked inside her, but she inhaled, held the

breath in her lungs. This wasn't her fault, but *damn*. They had to make decisions. And the main person who needed to be here—the one responsible—was absent, leaving them holding the bag. As usual.

"I know this, Athena," her mother snapped, then stretched out a hand, circling Athena's wrist. "I'm sorry, honey. I didn't mean to yell at you. This is…a mess. If this is true—"

"It is," Athena ground out.

"Then it's a mess and we need to take a minute and figure out how to address it."

"As a family." Athena stared at her mother, who glanced down at her lap. "Mom," she said, voice hardening. "As. A. Family."

"Why did Nico come by and tell you about this? What's his interest in it?" Winnie demanded.

"Mom—"

"Athena, please," her mother said, tone soft but brooking no argument. "Why did Nico tell you this? Why is this his business?"

She sighed, carefully choosing her words. "He proposed a…bargain. If I do a favor for him, he offered to pay off the debt."

Winnie jerked straight, a gasp tumbling from her lips. Hope flared in her eyes. "What?" She surged forward, clasping both of Athena's hands in her own. "You're kidding me? Why would he do that? Did you say yes?"

"What? No, I didn't say yes." Athena lurched to her feet, snatching free of her mother's desperate grip. Rubbing her hands together, she tried to rid her skin of that grasping sensation.

Or is that disgust you're trying to scrub clean?

As soon as the disloyal question popped into her head, she forced her arms to her sides, pacing away from the couch. From her mother.

"Athena," Winnie murmured.

"No, Mom." She pumped her hands in the air as if warding off whatever was bound to come out of her mother's mouth. Because instinct warned her she wouldn't like it.

"What does he want you to do? Is it illegal?"

"No, of course not," Athena said, tone sharp, but she immediately softened it. "Morally questionable, maybe, but not criminal." She glanced at her mother, frowning. "Forget it, Mom. I already told him I wouldn't do it."

"You won't tell me what it is?" Winnie quietly asked.

"No." Athena crossed her arms over her chest, uncertain why she felt...protective of Nico.

That proposal was so ridiculous, so filled with bitterness, that she wanted no part of it. There's no way she could get involved with something like that and not come away tainted. But his story didn't belong to her, so it wasn't hers to tell. She'd never even shared the truth about his parentage with her family. Nico Morgan might've broken her heart but she'd kept his secrets. And she had no plans to betray them now.

"It doesn't matter," she continued. "Now we have to—"

"How can you say that?" Her mother pushed to her feet, her fingers twisting in front of her. "How does it *not* matter? This is our lifeline, our way out. You know as well as I do your brother doesn't have that kind of money. If he did, he wouldn't have taken out that loan in the first place. Your father and I certainly don't. And we cannot lose Mama's bakery. It was her pride and joy, her everything. She loved..." She broke off. "We can't lose Evans," she finished on a cracked whisper.

"I can't, Mom," Athena whispered back. Desperation and...grief yawning deep inside. "What about Randall? Aren't you even going to ask him to step up, to take responsibility for this? He's threatened Evans, but once again..."

She didn't finish the sentence. Couldn't. A snarled ball of anger, sorrow and frustration lodged in her throat and she couldn't speak around it. She studied her mother's face, hoping she'd spy something there to bely her words.

But she found nothing. Nothing except what she expected.

"We're family, Athena. This is what family does. We have each other's back."

"Right," she whispered. Except, why couldn't she remember the last time they'd had *her* back?

Essentially disinherited.

Depended on to shoulder the responsibility of the family business.

Expected to give and give and give without complaint.

And she did it all.

She was so fucking tired of being the perfect, hungry-for-love daughter.

Turning away from her mother's dark, pleading gaze, Athena crossed the room to the dormant fireplace. Framed photos crowded the mantel. Black-and-white, cracked with age. Color and obviously more recent. But all family. And in almost all of them, Mama. Glory

Evans, the matriarch of the Evans family. The linchpin that had held them all together.

Winnie and Marcel Evans had adopted one-year-old Athena, and though she didn't share their DNA, she'd never viewed them as anything other than her parents. Other adopted children experienced that need to search for their biological parents, but she never had. Winnie and Marcel had been it for her—all she'd ever needed. And Mama... Well, Mama had been even more. No, she might not be an Evans by blood, but the bond she'd shared with her grandmother had run deeper than with any of her other grandchildren. Even deeper than with her own daughter.

Baking.

Athena had stood at her grandmother's knee with her toy bowls and spoons, pretending to mix ingredients, watching Mama until she'd been old enough to exchange the pretend eggs, flour and sugar for the real things. Their love for creating in the kitchen had resulted in not just new recipes but a relationship cemented by respect, acceptance and adoration.

God, she missed her.

Reaching out, Athena stroked a finger down one of the last pictures of Mama. Last year, on her birthday, with all of them surrounding her. Mom, Dad, Randall and his family. Athena and Kira, her younger sister. All of them grinned huge, celebrating another year of life for the woman they all loved and revered. Little had they known she would be gone in three short months.

Athena's gaze switched to a black-and-white photo. Glory and her husband, Thomas, standing in front of the newly opened Evans Bakery in 1962. They'd withstood lean times, threats for committing the sin of being a Black-owned business. They'd enjoyed success and survived the death of an owner, Thomas, long before Athena joined the Evans family. And through it all, Glory persevered, never closing Evans Bakery's doors.

And Athena couldn't allow them to close either.

Or allow anyone else to shut them.

Closing her eyes, she dropped her arm to her side.

She was going to do it. She was going to accept Nico's proposal.

But not for Randall. Not even for her mother.

She would do it for her grandmother.

Turning back to Winnie, she said, "Fine. I'll do it."

"Oh, Athena." Relief washed over her expression. "That's wonderful. Thank—"

"No, Mom." Athena shook her head. "I'm sorry. I don't mean to disrespect you. But please, don't thank me. I don't think I can handle that right now. Because I need to be clear, and you need to be clear as well. You're refusing to go to your son, the one who placed the bakery in jeopardy and demand he be accountable for his actions. That's it. And you won't do it. You'd rather ask—*beg*—me to take responsibility for him. Again. Even knowing it's placing me in an uncomfortable position. Involving me with a person who, by your own admission, you don't even care for. But the alternative—allowing Randall to face consequences—is abhorrent to you."

Never had she felt more expendable than she did in this moment.

"Honey, I love you," her mother whispered, extending a trembling hand. "You're so strong, and you know how your brother is…"

Athena took a step back and held her hand up. "One thing you need to understand, whether you tell Randall or not. I'm not doing this for him. And as much as I love you, Mom, I'm not going to Nico for you either. I'm doing this for Mama and her legacy, for Evans." Hiking her chin, she added, "And you'll need to do something to get Randall into the bakery. Because I can't save his behind *and* show up every morning at the store and work all day. It's your decision to spin whatever story you want, but he's going to need to step up."

Winnie nodded. "I'll do it."

Athena glanced away, mouth twisting. Her mother probably meant that. Literally. She wouldn't be surprised to find out Winnie showed up at the bakery tomorrow instead of Randall. Exhaling, Athena stared down at the floor, suddenly tired.

"I'll be in touch," she murmured and headed toward the front door.

"Athena, I—"

"Mom, I'll be in touch," she repeated.

Without risking a look at her mother, not when a whirlwind of emotions whipped at her, she exited her childhood home.

And for the first time since she'd entered it as a girl, she was unsure when she would be comfortable returning to it.

Because for the first time, it didn't feel like home.

Three

Why had Athena believed it would be simple to waltz into a downtown Boston office building and request to see a billionaire? On the twenty-minute drive here, the ten-minute search for an available spot in the parking deck and the seven-minute walk to the high-rise where Brightstar Holdings LLC occupied one of the top floors, she'd convinced herself it would be easy.

It seemed knowing how said billionaire sounded when he came deep inside you wasn't enough to gain access to him.

Not that she'd tried to explain that to the security guard currently staring at her as if she had mayhem on her mind.

"I'm sorry, ma'am," the dark-haired guard said for the third time. "But unless you have an appointment with Mr. Morgan—and according to his assistant, you do not—it's not possible for you to go up and see him today. I would suggest calling his office, scheduling an appointment, then returning at a later date."

The *"As for today, you're not getting past me,"* went left unsaid but she heard it loud and clear.

Sighing, she jerked open her purse and removed her cell. It'd been three years, but he probably hadn't changed his phone number. Nico hadn't been a fan of change. She doubted *that* had changed either. Not delving into why she hadn't erased his number from her contacts list, she pulled up his information and pressed Call. One ring. Two rings. As the fourth ring started, disappointment slicked through her. But just before she lowered the phone, a deep, smooth voice echoed in her ear.

"Athena?"

It appeared she wasn't the only one who hadn't removed old contacts.

"Yes," she said, glancing away from the security guard. "I'm downstairs in your office building at the security desk. Sorry for showing up without an appointment, but I need to speak with you about...about yesterday."

A beat of silence. Then, "Give the guard your phone."

She complied, extending the cell toward the other man. "It's for you."

Eyeing her, he accepted it. "Yes?" From one second to the next, his expression shifted from suspicious to stunned to contrite edged in panic. "Yes, sir. Right away. Thank you, sir." The guard passed the phone back to her. "He'd like to talk to you."

She pressed it to her ear. "Hello?"

"He's going to escort you upstairs." A pause. "And Athena?"

"Yes."

"I'm assuming the reason you're here isn't to give a repeat performance of yesterday's conversation."

She ground her teeth together, needing to unclench her jaw before saying, "No."

"Follow him. I'll see you in a few minutes."

The call ended, and she tried—and failed—to suppress a shiver at the ominous silence in her ear. Whether that shiver originated from trepidation or excitement? Well, she'd think about that later. When she wasn't headed up to the lion's den.

"Goodbye to you, too," she muttered, tucking the phone back in her purse. Turning to the guard, she smiled. "I've been ordered to follow you."

A gleam of humor lit his eyes as he slid the log-in book toward her. "If you'll sign in first, I'll take you upstairs to the Brightstar executive offices."

"Thank you."

Moments later, she stepped into the elevator with the guard, and as the doors soundlessly closed, she couldn't help but compare her surroundings to those of three years ago. When she'd dated Nico, his offices had been housed in a beautiful brick building in the Back Bay area. He'd been a millionaire then, the holding company he'd founded at twenty-four considered one of the fastest growing and wealthiest of the decade. An online search had provided a ton of information on him—and nothing personal.

Nico Morgan, Boston native, graduate of both MIT and Stanford University with multiple degrees in business management. With the assistance of investors, he'd founded Brightstar Holdings LLC at twenty-four years old and earned his first million at twenty-six. By twenty-nine, the business had expanded from not only holding the controlling stock in other companies under the parent entity, but Brightstar owned real estate, patents, trademarks and other assets. And other than a few on-dits and photos about who he'd been seen with, emerging from this restaurant or that gallery opening, that'd been it. Nothing else.

All the information about his past—his love and respect for his mother, the identity of his father—had come directly from him. Even now, as she rode up this pillar of glass and steel to his high-rise offices, awe shimmered inside her that Nico, a man who guarded his privacy tighter than the Hope Diamond's security detail, had shared parts of himself with her. Of course, that had been when she'd been so in love he could do no wrong. That had been her excuse. What'd been his? Momentary lapse in judgment triggered by bone-liquefying sex?

Yes. Putting the kibosh on thoughts of sex when about to meet said man who'd redefined the meaning of it seemed like a fabulous idea.

Swallowing a sigh, she instead focused on what she'd say to him. And just how much crow she could digest, since not twenty-four hours earlier she'd basically kicked him and his proposal out of her bakery.

God, this was going to be painful. Especially since crow tasted nothing like red velvet cupcakes.

The elevator slid to a stop and the door opened to a well-appointed lobby. A light wood—with serene blues and dark greens encompassed the decor's theme and lent the space a calming effect. Couches, tables and beautiful art of sweeping landscapes occupied half the room, and a wide, circular desk of the same wood claimed one corner. The effect exuded wealth and exclusivity while also inspiring confidence in the abilities of the personnel behind those closed doors to the left of the desk.

Oh yes, though her time of researching him online had passed, the new address, the atmosphere that reeked of money—it all telegraphed just how well Nico had done in the last few years.

"This way, Ms. Evans." The guard guided her toward the young man rising from his seat behind the desk. "Mr. Morgan asked me to bring up his guest, a Ms. Athena Evans. He's expecting her."

"Yes." The young man, whose nameplate identified him as Paul Landon, said, "I can take Ms. Evans back. Thank you." Turning to Athena, he nodded. "If you'll come with me."

She moved toward the closed double doors but paused to offer the security guard a smile, and a warm one this time. "Thank you for your help."

"You're welcome." Dipping his chin, he headed for the elevators, and she…

Well, she headed for her fate.

Paul led her through the doors and she stepped into an open, surprisingly bright area. Desks and small sitting nooks dotted either side of the hall. She passed a wall of windows and a large conference room with black leather chairs and small computer monitors mounted on the table like soldiers in front of them. Offices, some with open doors and others with closed, claimed the rest of the space, and at the far end, Paul paused in front of a closed one.

With a quick knock, he opened the door and stepped inside.

"Mr. Morgan, Ms. Evans to see you."

"Thank you, Paul. Please shut the door behind you." Nico rose from behind his desk, and her gaze zeroed in on him.

She didn't see or hear Paul leave behind her. Nico commandeered every sense, creating a vacuum in the room so everything centered on him. Yesterday had been like falling into a vortex of *him*, and today was no different.

How many times had she lost herself in that onyx gaze? How eyes so dark could blaze so hot had been an enigma she'd never solved. She'd just enjoyed the burn. Even now, as he rounded his desk and stalked across the cavernous office, that black stare roamed over her face, dipping to her mint green sleeveless blouse and high-waisted, emerald, wide-legged pants. Her exposed skin tingled, as if sunburned, and it required every ounce of restraint she possessed not to skim her fingertips over the affected area. She refused to acknowledge—even to herself—that he affected her.

Affected her. Hah. Such a poor word to describe the…the gravitational pull that seemed to wrench her in his direction.

She wanted to pounce on the excuse of a three-year absence intensifying his magnetism, but that would be a lie. This *thing* between them had always been powerful, electric. From the first time they'd met at a restaurant opening to the last time she'd walked out of his penthouse…

And he let her go.

Her birth parents. Nico. And even, in some ways, her adopted parents.

Why was it so easy for people to let her go?

What was it about her that…?

No, she'd traveled that road, pitted with doubts and insecurities, so many times. None of the sharp curves and ditches remained a mystery. She had filled those potholes with enough tears to flood them out. And for what? Nothing changed. So she did what she always did.

Kept moving forward.

Kept…fixing.

Which was what brought her here today. Fixing a mess.

"Thank you for seeing me, Nico," she said, surprised and grateful her voice held steady when her thoughts ping-ponged all over the place, taking her emotions with them.

"Call it curiosity."

He cocked his head, sliding his hands in the front pockets of his pants, the move spreading his dark gray suit jacket open. A light gray and black tie bisected the white shirt stretching over his wide chest, and she jerked her gaze back to his face. Heat poured into her throat and cheeks. *Please, God, don't let him have noticed. Or at the very least, let him pretend he didn't notice.*

But this was Nico. Nothing got by him. And the arch of that dark eyebrow informed her he'd caught the slip.

Deny, deny, deny. Or ignore, ignore, ignore.

"Curious?" she parroted.

"About what could have possibly torn you from that bakery and caused you to come down here. To me."

...*Come down here. To me.*

That shouldn't have sounded like an erotic invitation. But from the syrupy lust pouring through her veins and the liquid heat gathering between her thighs, her body heard it as one.

There'd been a time when she hadn't needed permission to tunnel her fingers through the thick, black waves that framed his face. A time when those deep-set, obsidian eyes had glittered with pleasure as her lips mapped the fierce features of his face. Either a loving, meticulous sculptor or a mad, frantic artist could be blamed for the broad brow, slashing cheekbones, arrogant blade of nose and the indecently lush mouth. The angles, slants and curves formed a work of art so harsh, so brutal, so sensual, a person vacillated between worshipping it or scurrying away.

With that tall, lean, powerful body, he reminded her of a wolf. Lethal, untamed, gorgeous and hungry. Always hungry for more, whether it was success, contracts, companies, revenge...her.

She shivered.

God, how he'd once been ravenous for her.

Her gaze dipped to his mouth, and a buzz like downing a fast shot of whiskey sizzled inside her. Glancing away, she focused on the sitting area with the couch, chairs and tables with a stunning view of the city and Boston Harbor as a backdrop.

"I need to speak with you about your...proposal from yesterday," she said.

"Look at me."

She jerked her attention back to him, the blunt demand brooking nothing less than obedience. And dammit, she gave it to him.

"I don't feel like having this conversation with the back of your head," he continued, his tone smooth, with a hint of steel. "Don't get shy now, Athena. Look me in the eyes and confess why you're here."

Shy.

Right. They both knew what he really meant. *Don't be a coward. Say the words.* Because he wanted them. He would feast on this pound of flesh.

Anger flashed inside her, so bright and hot she should be a pile of ash in front of him.

"You're enjoying this, aren't you?" she ground out.

"Yes." He inclined his head. "Now tell me why you're here."

She bared her teeth in a facsimile of a smile, spreading her arms wide. "Why, I'm here to whore myself."

Oh yes, she was being facetious, but in a way, the words struck too close to home. Bile churned in her belly. She was selling herself for her family.

God…

"Get out."

The cold order snatched her from her own head, and she blinked, staring at him. Noting the *furious* lines of his face, the gleam in his black eyes and the flattening of his full lips. She nearly stumbled back. Only pride kept her rooted, and that might very well be her downfall. But it couldn't prevent a tingle of foreboding from tripping over the nape of her neck.

"What?" she asked, shaking her head.

"Get out," he repeated. "If this is your play, I'm not

interested. Because I'm not your family. They're in the victimization business, not me. They make a fucking profession of playing the victims and expecting you to be their savior. I'm not going there with you. I offered you a bargain. Accept the terms or don't. Those are your choices. But this sacrificial lamb bullshit? Do it with them, not me."

His words—no, his accusation—pummeled the breath from her lungs. She stood there, bruised and shaken by the ugly truth in them. She'd wanted the choice to be taken from her, to be a victim so she could have no blame in this situation. When in truth, she had as much accountability as her mother, as the rest of her family. Because she could've said no. She could've tracked her brother down in whatever bed, bar or hole he'd hidden in and ordered him to straighten out what he'd fucked up.

But she hadn't. She done what she always did.

Raced to the rescue. Or trudged, in this case, but the result was the same.

Trouble, that one. And if you're not careful, he'll take you down in the mud while he comes out smelling like a rose.

That hadn't been Nico's warning about Randall, but Mama's. And as much as Athena longed to yell at Randall for screwing up and being so damn selfish again, and at Nico for, well…everything past and present, she couldn't. Wouldn't. Because in the end, this wasn't about either one of them.

This was about her grandmother and the legacy she'd worked over fifty years to ensure succeeded. If Athena had to save her brother's ass from the fire one more time and enter a devil's bargain to do it, then it was a small sacrifice.

It was the least she could do for the woman who'd loved her unconditionally and never made her feel any less of an Evans.

"You're right," she murmured, catching the flare of surprise in Nico's dark eyes.

But in the next moment, his gaze became hooded, suspicious.

"I'm right," he drawled, arching an eyebrow. "Forgive me if I'm stunned—and skeptical—of this sudden agreement. Especially since your very presence here contradicts the words coming out of your mouth." He cocked his head, that intense stare probing, cutting. "If you're here to assume the role of the walking wounded, there's the door. On the other hand, if you're going to own your decision, then tell me what that is and let's move forward."

"I get it, Nico," she quietly said.

"Do you?" He softly snorted. "That would be a first."

"I offended you, and I'm sorry."

He studied her for several long moments. And those black eyes revealed nothing of his thoughts. She'd always resented—and admired—that talent.

"Why are you here?" he finally asked.

Sand seemed to coat her tongue, but she swallowed, barreling past the suffocating sensation. "To ask you if the offer to cover my brother's loan is still open. If it is, I've changed my mind, and I'd like to accept it."

"Not offer, Athena. Bargain. Proposal. Because I want something from you for that three hundred thousand dollars, plus interest. Are you willing to meet those terms?"

She parted her lips but before she could answer, he stepped forward, his hands sliding out of his pockets. His big body glided with a grace and power that sent a frisson of excitement skittering through her. Of their own volition, her thighs squeezed as if remembering embracing those lean hips as he moved over her, thrusting deep inside, claiming her...

"Should I spell out those terms for you?" he asked, crossing the office and not stopping until only inches separated them. He didn't touch her, but that achingly familiar scent of sandalwood and soap wrapped around her, teasing her senses and bombarding her with memories better locked away. Was breathing really necessary? "I'll pay off your brother's debt, saving your precious bakery. And in return, you're going to pretend to be my fiancée. My lover, Athena. In front of Cain and Achilles Farrell and Kenan Rhodes and their significant others, we will be two people hopelessly in love, who look seconds from finding the nearest corner to fuck in. I don't give a damn if you begrudge every breath I take, when we're in front of them—in public, period—for the next three months, you will make everyone believe there's no other man you want." His head lowered until their breath nearly mingled, mated. "No other cock you need inside you."

She should be disgusted at his language, at the infiltration of her personal space when they'd ceased being *that* to one another long ago. Should... Instead lust shimmered between them, thick and heavy. She *inhaled* it. But just under that desire pulsed the resentment he mentioned.

That, too, should've disappeared after three years. But it beat within her, making its presence known. And with each throb in her veins and ache between her thighs, that anger grew.

"You couldn't even say that word aloud when we were together," she whispered, trying and failing to keep the bitterness out of her voice. Not so with her. She'd been the first, and the last, to say "I love you," in their relationship.

"Fuck?" His gaze flicked to her mouth, then returned to her eyes. "Not true. I used it quite frequently and creatively if memory serves."

"I'm glad I amuse you." Because she couldn't draw in one more sandalwood and fresh soap-infused breath, she stepped back and to the side, not caring if he interpreted it as a retreat. She needed space. "And no worries, Nico," she said, curving her mouth into a tight smile. "I have three hundred thousand reasons to bring my best performance."

"And I intend to get my money's worth," he murmured, and damn if that didn't sound like a threat…or a promise. "Out of curiosity—" he stalked back to his desk and hiked a hip on the corner "—who begged you to come to me? Your parents? Your brother? Or do they even know you're here?"

"I have terms of my own," she said, avoiding his question. "My family is off-limits. We don't talk about them. We don't involve them. From here on out, this is just between you and me."

"Still the fierce protector." The corner of his mouth

quirked high, but it contained more than a hint of derision. "A shame they've never thought to return the favor."

"Off. Limits," she ground out. "Second, before I begin…anything, I want a contract spelling out that you will clear Randall's debt regardless of whether your plans come to fruition or not."

"One would think you didn't trust me." He scoffed, shrugging a shoulder. "Done. You're not the only one with trust issues, baby girl. The contract will be in your in-box this evening. With an NDA. Which will pertain to your family as well. Because I don't want them in my business any more than you do."

Shit. She rubbed her fingertips over her forehead. "That's a problem. I already told my mother about the loan and your offer to pay it off. I didn't go into the details of the arrangement you proposed, but she is aware of your involvement."

"Well, that answers my question, doesn't it?" His eyes narrowed on her. "Your mother offered you up like a lamb to the lion." He chuckled and the dark sound held no trace of humor. "Do you ever get tired, Athena? Martyrdom must be so exhausting."

"You're already violating my first stipulation," she warned, even as her mind railed, *Yes, dammit, it is.*

He waved a hand. "Right. My apologies." He dipped his head, although nothing about his flinty gaze or grim smile relayed regret. "I'll send your mother a nondisclosure agreement as well."

Athena flinched. "Are you serious? You're sending an *NDA* to my *mother*?"

"You're damn right. I trust her even less than I trust

you. She possesses a blind spot the size of Longfellow Bridge when it comes to your brother."

She wished she could argue.

"Anything else?" he asked. "Any more provisions you wish to add?"

"Yes." She met his gaze, even though a small voice whispered that she was pushing it. "About this plan of yours…"

He didn't move from his perch on the desk and yet his body seemed to loom closer. The space that separated them suddenly didn't feel adequate. But she stood her ground.

"Yes?"

She didn't fool herself. That almost gentle "yes" did not invite further inquiry.

"I don't want to be involved in anything that will hurt someone," she said. "I'm not going to let you make me a party to that."

Now he did move. Slowly, his big frame unfolded, and her breath caught in her throat at his carnal grace. He was sex in motion. She couldn't do anything but watch him. Take him in.

"After Brightstar had been in business for three years, Barron came to my office. Smiling. Proud. Bragging that he was my father. He acted as if he was responsible for my hard work, my success. Even told me I got my killer instinct from him."

Athena's fingers fluttered to her throat, circling the column as if she could capture the gasp there. Nico had never mentioned meeting his father. Why hadn't he…?

"Nico," she breathed.

"I told him I knew exactly who he was and to go

fuck himself. That went over well." A faint smile, void of humor, ghosted across his mouth. "His response was to try and ruin my company. But I'd expected that and had been prepared. When he couldn't destroy my business or reputation, Barron made it personal. My mother worked for a department store at the time—Bromberg's. Farrell International owned the chain, and he had her fired. Not that she needed the money, but Mom enjoyed her job. None of that mattered to Barron. He made sure she was escorted out by security and humiliated, just to get back at me for not needing him."

"I'm so sorry." She shook her head in disgust. "Rhoda was such a proud woman. I can't even imagine how…" She gave her head another shake. "I'm sorry," she repeated, softer this time.

"Barron wielded that fucking company like his personal weapon. It was his everything. His lover. His power. His legacy. The only thing he cared about. Even more than his family—his sons. And just like he came after what—who—I loved most in this world, I'm going after what he cared about. Even if he's not here to see it. He would've sacrificed the happiness, the welfare and peace of anyone who got in his way if it meant protecting his reputation or Farrell International. By the time I'm done, neither will remain." His chest rose and fell on his deep breaths. On his anger. "That's *my* legacy."

"And your brothers?" she whispered. "What about them? I looked them up. Except for Cain, none of them knew Barron or grew up with him. And Achilles appears to have a similar background as yours. You might have more in common with them than you think. Have you met them? Have you even considered that you might be punishing them in this plan?"

"This isn't about them, nor is this a family reunion. Just as they have no idea I even exist, I have no affection or loyalty toward them. They're men who have the misfortune of sharing the same DNA as me. That's it." He slashed his hand through the air. "The fact is they were blackmailed into overseeing that company. A company that is a monument to a man who didn't give a fuck about people in life and gave even less about them in death. No, Athena, I'm not walking away. Not until Farrell International lies in rubble. And you have a choice. Stay, knowing what's ahead. Or leave. But if you leave this time, there's no second chance."

She could go. And her grandmother's bakery would go with her. He wasn't the only one who had a legacy on the line.

"I'm staying," she said. "But you should know that I'm not going to stop trying to convince you that there's a better path than the one you've set yourself on. Revenge, Nico…" She spread her hands wide, palms up. "You can't possibly believe you'll escape the fallout. And I know you can't—or won't—believe this, but I don't want to see you hurt. And this has pain written all over it."

Something flickered in his eyes, and if possible his face hardened even more. The curve of his lips did nothing to soften it.

"You're right. I don't believe it." He angled his head, and an edge sharpened his silken tone. "Let's be clear, Athena, we're pretending to be an engaged couple who cares for one another. It's a pretense that doesn't spill over into reality. There's no need for method acting. Unless…"

His hooded gaze dropped once more to her mouth. *Dammit*, she nearly sank her teeth into her bottom lip. She managed to prevent that telltale action but could do nothing about the catch of breath in her lungs. God, if he heard that… His glittering eyes shifted back to hers. *Oh yes.* He'd most definitely *heard.*

"I don't want to hear one damn lie from your mouth, but if you want to rehearse other aspects of our performance, I believe in perfection."

The low rumble of his voice stroked over her exposed skin, caressed her breasts, leaving her nipples beaded. Her belly pulled so tight, she swallowed a whimper, attempting to ignore the throbbing ache deep in her sex. And failing.

She hated his effect on her. Hated how…empty she felt.

Hated how she needed him to fill her.

Only him.

"Next stipulation," she whispered. "We save all public displays of affection for the public."

"And you save your pretty lies for yourself."

They stared at one another, only the jagged rasp of her breath punctuating the silence.

You left me first!

The scream ricocheted off her skull. Despair threatened to sweep her feet out from under her, because she'd believed she'd moved past this. *This.* This right here was why she didn't—couldn't—allow the door to her past with Nico to creak open. It jeopardized all her hard-won control and contentment.

He'd *devastated* her.

In *his* narrative, he was the injured party. She'd constantly chosen her family over him. She'd walked out on him. But he'd abandoned *them* long before she'd left his penthouse that day. At some point, she'd convinced herself it was okay that he'd never love her, even though she'd given him her heart. But in the end, investing all of herself into a relationship, into a man who refused to do the same, had drained her. She couldn't do it any longer. But Nico had only seen her returning home as once more allowing her family to manipulate her.

And he'd let her go.

He hadn't come after her. Because his feelings for her had limits.

He wasn't so different from everyone else in her life, after all.

"Three months," she whispered.

"Three months," he said. "Then we go back to business as usual. Where I don't exist in your perfect world and you're no longer a part of mine. But until then," he moved forward, blocking out everything in the room but *him*, "you are mine and I'm yours. Better learn how to act like it."

"And you?" she demanded, hiking up her chin. "Can you *act like it*?"

What the hell are you doing?

He didn't answer her.

Then again, yes, he did.

Nico shifter closer, until the lapels of his suit jacket grazed the ruffles on the front of her blouse. And then closer still. Until the unyielding granite of his chest pressed against her breasts. This time, the whimper in her throat clawed free. Mortified, she closed her eyes.

But when that only amplified the lust crackling in her veins, she quickly opened them again.

Damn. It'd been *so long*.

So long since she'd been touched.

So long since a man's body had aligned with hers, thighs bracketing hers, dick—*oh God*—dick nudging her stomach.

No, no. Not any man. *This man*. Nico.

The backs of his fingers trailed down her cheek, and a whisper of air shuddered from between her lips. Nico leaned back, staring down into her face. He rubbed a thumb over her bottom lip, seeming not to care about messing up her lipstick or that it would stain his skin. The caress wasn't gentle. He pressed the tender flesh against her teeth, and she fucking loved it. Loved the messiness of it, the eroticism of it.

Just loved that he touched her.

"Can I act like I want you? Like my hands itch to tangle in these beautiful curls? Or that my cock gets hard just from me touching this rude as fuck mouth and remembering how well you use it? Or that my body is on the verge of taking you down to this floor and covering you like the animal you think I am?"

He slipped the tip of his thumb between her lips. Her tongue barely dabbed the skin before he withdrew.

Nico stepped back. Taking his heat. The carnal pall he'd dropped over them. She shivered in the sudden loss of temperature. Blinked against the abrupt return to reality.

Oh shit.

She met his narrowed, assessing gaze and humiliation crept into her face.

"I think I have it covered," he said, arching a dark eyebrow.

He'd played her. Of course he'd noticed her physical reaction to him—the man missed nothing—and he'd played her.

Well, screw him.

"Yes, I kind of got the notice." She deliberately lowered her gaze to the still-hard erection ruining the pleat of his suit pants.

"Touché." Without trying to cover the evidence of his arousal, he crossed his arms over his chest. "Are we in agreement, Athena? No more terms to discuss?"

"Yes." She inhaled—then exhaled. And sealed her fate. "And no."

"Good." He nodded. His voice lowered. "Do you want to shake on it?"

She didn't, and he didn't expect her to; it's why he offered.

And it's why she crossed the space between them, hand extended. Surprise flared in his eyes, and maybe a glimmer of admiration. She didn't give a damn about his admiration. But the satisfaction that careened inside her at the surprise? That was sweet.

Still…she braced herself. Because pride might be driving her forward but it didn't fool her.

When her palm slid across his, those long fingers wrapping tightly around hers, she couldn't prepare for the punch of lust that barreled into her like a runaway freight train. Hell, this was ridiculous. She'd just had his cock on her stomach, for God's sakes. But his hand surrounding hers had her sex clenching hard.

Damned if he'd know it, though.

Schooling her expression, she met his gaze, even gave his hand a firm squeeze before letting go. And ordered herself not to scrub away the tingle in her palm.

"The contract will be in your in-box this afternoon, Athena. As soon as you sign and return it, we begin. Don't even think of walking away."

Again. He didn't say it, but it echoed between them loud and clear.

"I wouldn't dream of it."

She turned and left. But she would be back.

Three hundred thousand dollars and her grandmother's dream ensured that.

Four

Nico stepped from the back of the town car, absently buttoning his tuxedo jacket, his gaze focused on the three-story apartment building in front of him. The Cambridge condominium was new; Athena had lived in a duplex near her family's Dorchester home when they'd first started dating. He glanced around the quiet street, noting the designs of the other buildings that differed enough to prevent a cookie-cutter view. A bicycle rack outside one downstairs balcony. A small garden in front of another. A waterfall of hanging plants and colorful flowers decorating yet another. The neighborhood seemed nice, peaceful.

What the hell was Athena doing here?

Moving onto the curb, he again checked the discreet black iron number on the building, then climbed the covered stairs to the second level. Verifying he had the right apartment, he knocked on the green door with the gold three in the center.

Impatience flickered inside him, and he ruthlessly smothered it. He couldn't afford to be anything but clearheaded. Especially tonight. Tonight would be the commencement of years of planning. Tonight he would make his first overt move into Barron's inner circle—the one he'd created after his death. Nico couldn't make mistakes, not with the men who were his half brothers.

Half brothers.

His mouth twisted. As did something buried deep in his chest.

Nico had followed Cain and Achilles Farrell and Kenan Rhodes over the last nine months. The three men who'd once been strangers seemed close and supportive of one another. They definitely worked well together. Farrell International had thrived under their joint ownership, even in just these few months. With Cain's experience with the company, Achilles's technology knowledge and recent acquisition of a gaming software design company, and Kenan's marketing expertise and recent revitalization of the Bromberg's department store, they'd exceeded the board's and shareholders' expectations.

Had Barron foreseen that? Or had he wanted his offspring to crash and burn without him at the helm? Hard to tell with that bastard. Probably the latter. But Barron hadn't counted on them bonding like real brothers.

I have no affection or loyalty toward them. They're men who have the misfortune of sharing the same DNA as me.

The words he'd hurled at Athena a week earlier in

his office paraded through his head. For a moment, he'd frozen, fearing she'd caught a trace of bitterness in his voice. For all his life, it'd been just him and his mother, until she'd died. No father to call on for advice. No brothers to lean on. He hadn't cared.

Until Athena asked him about his half brothers.

That had always been her superpower and his kryptonite. She'd made him *fucking* feel. It'd terrified him even as it'd brought him to his knees. Only for her.

And what had she done while he'd been there? Torn his figurative throat out.

She'd taught him a valuable lesson that no college professor, cunning businessman or even his so-called father had.

Vulnerability and trust were risks not worth the high cost.

Only a fool repeated the same mistake when the losses damn near wiped him out.

He wasn't a fool.

So being alone—didn't bother him.

Not when the alternative meant letting another person tear a hole open in him.

Again.

The condominium door opened, and his resolve took a direct hit.

Fuck.

It required every ounce of the icy control he was known for not to crowd her back into her apartment and peel that cocktease of a dress from her body.

Not push deep into that tight, wet warmth he remembered.

"What's wrong?" She frowned, glancing down and

skimming her palms over sweetly rounded hips and slender thighs. "You can't complain. This is one of the dresses you sent over. Which, by the way, I'm sure you didn't mean to imply that I'm not capable of choosing clothes for myself."

"I'm not an idiot." For choosing this dress? Yes, he was. "I wouldn't dare to presume that. Or tell you if I did." He nodded toward the entryway. "Are you going to allow me in?"

She hesitated, and he didn't know whether to be offended or amused. Before he could decide, she shrugged a bare shoulder and shifted to the side.

He didn't try to quell the curiosity that swept through him as he entered. When he'd known her years ago, her tastes had ranged from bohemian chic to eclectic—a nicer term for damn near weird. Athena would conscript him into going on shopping jaunts to the Cambridge Antique Market to hunt down what she called "treasures." Sometimes, her grandmother would join them, and the two of them could go for hours, while Nico trailed behind, their glorified caddy. They had been some of the happiest times he'd shared with her.

But the atrocities and oddities that had ended up in her little Dorchester apartment? Those he could've gone his whole life without seeing.

Stepping inside this new place, he surveyed the open living area that flowed from one room to another, the only partition an exposed brick wall separating the kitchen from the rest of the home. A hall branched off from the entrance of the sunken living room, leading to, he assumed, bedrooms and bathrooms. As he moved farther into the condo, he spotted the glass French doors leading to a balcony.

But these details didn't catch his attention. The total lack of personality—*her* personality—did. He scanned the area once more, certain he'd missed…something. Anything that betrayed the vibrant person with so much vitality that it emanated from her, even into her kooky decor.

Yet *she* was missing.

What happened?

The question weighed on his tongue like a massive boulder. A band constricted around his chest. His palms tingled, the muscles in his arms tensed, preparing to… what? Grab her? Drag her close, fold around her and hold her tight? Rub up and down that ramrod straight spine and demand to know what the fuck happened to strip her of joy? Because he sensed with a certainty that had earned him his first million that's what had happened. The uninhibited glee with which she used to decorate her place had been her safe, happy space.

What—or who—had stolen that from her? And what did Nico need to tear down, to raze to the ground to return it to her?

"Nico?"

The sound of his name wrapped in her sultry voice yanked him back. The three years she'd been out of his life were her business, not his. And opening that door only invited a trouble he had no desire to entertain.

Three months.

Three months, with rules. And then she would be gone, disappearing like smoke once more. Only this time, he would be the one extinguishing the "relation-ship."

"You look lovely," he said, unable to contain the edge of a growl that roughened his voice.

"This old thing?" she drawled, but again, she rubbed her hands down the emerald lace gown, the nervous gesture belying her snarky tone.

He could've told her to stop fidgeting, that she had zero to worry about. That she was a goddamn vision. He could go into detail about how the wide off-the-shoulder straps emphasized the beauty of her breasts, lifting them and throwing him back into memories of when he had permission to cup their soft, firm weight.

Could tell her how the lace conformed to each perfect curve like a lover. Could express how that thigh-high slit offered him a seductive peek at her long, toned leg.

Could finish with how her crown of curls was the very picture of elegance. But it also had him battling the urge to remove each and every pin until those wild, gorgeous spirals filled his hands, tangled around his fingers.

Yes, he could inform her of all of that.

Instead, he glanced away from the temptation of her. "Are you ready to go?"

He felt her considering gaze on him rather than saw it. That's because he refused to meet it, like a coward. But if she glimpsed what he suspected he did a damn poor job of concealing... No, until he got his shit to-gether, he'd avoid that too-perceptive scrutiny.

"I am. Let me just get my wrap."

When she strode over to the couch, he deemed it safe

to turn around. He watched the subtle, sensual sway of her hips and ass.

It was going to be a long night.

She picked up a length of matching satin material off the back of the sofa, then headed back in his direction.

"Here, let me." He took the wrap and settled it around her shoulders because manners dictated he had to, not just so he could inhale her sugar, vanilla and warm skin scent.

"I'll admit, the stylist chose well. Thank you for arranging all of this," she murmured. "I didn't mean to sound ungrateful."

Stylist. Right. Here's where he could've admitted that he'd personally chosen all the gowns sent over, including this one because it'd made him think of the green in her hazel eyes, but he trapped that confession behind a clenched jaw.

"You're welcome."

He stepped back.

Touching her would be a part of the pretense, and if his reaction to her now was anything to go by, this night would be far more difficult than he'd first believed.

Mentally, he chuckled at himself and it held no trace of humor. Hubris. He'd been accused of possessing more than his fair share a time or two. Not until this moment did he believe it. Because he'd thought being in Athena's presence, casually caressing her, hell, even looking at her, wouldn't affect him. Not after she'd betrayed him, abandoned him—abandoned *them*.

But he'd been laughably wrong.

If he was going to maintain any semblance of control

over this situation, then he had to pace himself. Which meant only touching her if he needed to.

Resolve hardening inside him, he headed toward her front door and stepped outside into the hot August night, waiting until she followed behind him and locked up her apartment. Nico waved away his driver, who'd exited the town car, and opened the rear door for Athena himself. Once she moved inside, he folded in after her.

Her warm, sweet scent permeated the interior, and he ground his teeth. When this was over, first thing he'd do was detail the car. Damned if every time he rode in his own vehicle her scent would haunt him like a ghost that refused to be exorcised.

Like his memories.

He silently growled at that unwanted reminder. And untrue. He hadn't spent the last three years mired in the past.

Can I act like I want you? Like my hands itch to tangle in these beautiful curls? Or that my cock gets hard just from me touching this rude as fuck mouth and remembering how well you use it? Or that my body is on the verge of taking you down to this floor and covering you like the animal you think I am?

Shit. That had been a monumental Freudian slip. But it didn't mean…fuck it.

"So, details about tonight," she said, her fingers going at each other on her lap, twisting and tangling. "What is this again? And what's our story? We didn't even nail down any backstory about how we met or our engagement? Every couple has a proposal story," she muttered, babbling.

Without permission from his brain—and in direct

defiance of the edict he'd just issued about no unnecessary touching—he covered her hands with one of his, stilling the agitated motion. Beside him, she stiffened, but he didn't remove his hand, even though a part of him yelled to do just that. They weren't *this*. He didn't give a fuck about soothing her. All he needed from her was to be convincing as his fiancée and make him appear nonthreatening to Cain and Achilles Farrell and Kenan Rhodes. Make him appear...human.

And yet...he still didn't remove his hand.

And she didn't slide hers out from under his.

"We're attending a party celebrating the renovation of the Bromberg's department store."

"I'd heard about the possible closing of the store," she said, frowning. "We all shopped there when I was younger. Not so much now, but it's definitely a part of my childhood and has been an institution in Boston for decades."

"Under Kenan Rhodes, it's being rebranded and modernized to not only appeal to its established customer base, but also invite a younger clientele. He proposed a fusion of classic and contemporary that makes sense. Which is why I voted to approve going forward with the project and invested in it." A small sound came from her direction and he turned, meeting her steady gaze. "What?"

"Nothing," she said.

He arched an eyebrow. "Which means something. I might regret asking this, but, Athena, what are you thinking?"

"Now I really want to tell you." She scowled, but neither the expression nor her tone contained much heat.

Angling her head, she studied him, the passing shadows not hiding the contemplation in her eyes. "If I'm not mistaken, I heard admiration in your voice for your brother. And I might not know much about the corporate side of business, but you're a shareholder of Farrell International. You could vote to approve the project without investing in it. You must believe in it."

Don't you look away from her. Don't fucking do it.

If he did, it would only encourage Athena and cement, in her mind, that her ideas were true. And they were the furthest from reality.

Irritation flickered in his chest, a flare that would only take a soft gust to blow into flame.

"I admire any businessman who can yield a return," he said, ice crackling from each word. "Nothing more, nothing less. To me, Kenan Rhodes is one of the owners of the company I plan to take over. Not a brother, not anything, in spite of your persistence in seeing what doesn't exist." He shook his head, letting loose a soft scoff. "I'm surprised, Athena. You, of all people, should've stopped believing in family reunions and happily-ever-afters long ago. Real life doesn't work like that."

"I should've stopped believing in family reunions because I'm adopted and my birth parents never came looking for me?" she murmured.

Damn. Oh *damn.* "No, Athena," he softly objected. "I didn't—"

"Or I should've stopped believing in happily-ever-afters because the relationship I had crashed and burned so badly that three years later I still bear the scorch marks?"

He went rigid, that flame leaping into a full-out fire. Tension punched into the car's interior, so dense, he could choke on it. Slowly, he withdrew his hand from hers, but he didn't remove his gaze from the emotions stealing over her expression. Fury. Defiance. Sorrow… Pain.

Those last two only stoked the heat razing a path across his sternum. She had no right to show him grief or hurt. None. *She'd* broken them. *She'd* thrown them away.

She'd deemed him unworthy of a place in her world. Like his father.

Horror pierced through the anger, and he scuttled away from that last thought as if it had spindly legs and venom.

He didn't need her. Didn't need the vulnerability she exposed in him.

"Yes," he finally said, convincing himself that her flinch didn't cause him pain. "Exactly." Then, because he couldn't let the first part of her assumption go, he flatly added, "I don't know why your birth parents put you up for adoption. It could be as simple as not wanting the responsibility of a newborn or as complicated as desiring to give a child they loved a better life. Or anything in between. What I do know is that the fact they haven't tried to reach out to you or find you has nothing to do with your worth as a person. You are the best thing those people ever created together, and as much as I don't see eye to eye with your adopted parents, that's one sentiment we probably agree on."

She stared at him, lips parted, surprise gleaming in her hazel eyes.

The same surprise echoed in him. He hadn't meant to say that, but he also refused to rescind it.

Ducking her head, her long chandelier earrings grazing the tops of her bared shoulders, she whispered, "Thank you."

He didn't reply. Several moments passed, the tension in the car no less thick but not as kinetic with emotion.

"So," she cleared her throat, "as for how we met? What are we going with?"

"The truth. We met three years ago but lost touch. Then we saw each other again when I came into the bakery. We reconnected. We'll just adjust the timeline. Instead of a week ago, we'll say four months. Everyone loves a whirlwind, second chance romance." He smiled, and it barely lifted the corner of his mouth. "If we stick as close to the truth as possible, there's less chance of messing up and we appear more believable."

"Have a lot of experience in deception, do we?" she mocked. Before he could reply, she flipped a hand over, holding it up. "Makes sense. But I think I'll leave out the 'pretend fiancée or lose your sixty-year business' part. Kind of takes the romantic shine off things."

He snorted. "Probably a good idea."

"What about our proposal?"

A throb set up in his temple. The memory that wavered across his mind should've dimmed with age and distance. Instead it popped up in front of his mind's eye, too clear, too vivid. Almost immediately, he ejected it. But not quickly enough. The footprint of it remained, and he briefly closed his eyes, dragging in a deep breath.

"Nico?" Athena asked.

"You decide. Doesn't matter to me."

The words emerged rough, terse, and he switched his gaze to the side window. *Dammit*. He clenched his jaw. If he didn't stop allowing the past to creep into the present, he wouldn't have to worry about Athena not holding up her end of this bargain. He'd wreck it. And he'd watched his mother struggle too long to fuck up now.

The rest of the ride passed in silence, and only when they stopped at the last light before Bromberg's did he reach inside his tuxedo jacket and remove a small, black box.

Passing it to her, he said, "Here. You're going to need this."

She stared down at the box, not immediately taking it from his palm. Just as he was about to utter her name, she blinked and he caught the slight tremble in her fingers as she picked it up and opened the lid.

The princess cut, five-carat diamond ring sat on a bed of black velvet and winked under the light that slanted into the car from the streetlamp. The jewelry exuded beauty, elegance and wealth.

And it was impersonal as hell.

He glanced at her, and an emotion he had no trouble identifying flickered over her face before she cleared it. Dismay. Panic.

Athena wanted that ring on her finger about as much as he desired to slide it on there.

How fucked-up was it that her obvious aversion had him ready to snatch the damn thing from the box, shove it on her finger and demand she wear it and like it?

Very.

"It's just a ring, Athena," he said, voice flat. "It's nothing but a necessary prop and means nothing."

Unlike another one for an aborted proposal a long time ago. But as it turned out, that had meant nothing, too.

"I know. I—" She stopped talking, her mouth thinning into a firm line. After another moment of peering at the jewelry as if it contained poison, she finally removed it from the box and slid it on with abrupt, economical movements. "You're right. Can't have a fiancée without a ring. Amateur mistake."

She turned and gazed out the window, and as if drawn by a relentless force, his scrutiny dropped to her lap where her hand rested. The diamond covered the width of her ring finger, staking an unmistakable claim that was false. Of all the deceptions he was ready to commit on behalf of meting out justice to a dead man, this one sat like ash in his mouth.

Jerking his attention from the lie of a ring, he stared straight ahead. In moments, they would arrive at Bromberg's, and the latest step in his plan—the most important besides quietly purchasing shares through shell companies and obtaining the majority—would commence. Focus was key. And not on the woman beside him.

"We're here," he announced as the town car slowed, entering the line of vehicles waiting to approach the front of the department store. "Are you ready, Athena?"

"To aid and abet you in duping your brothers and their women into trusting you so they're looking the other way as you blindside them with a hostile takeover?" She turned away from the window and flashed him a tight, humorless smile. "Sure. I'm ready, Nico."

Guilt flashed inside him. Guilt and shame. But as quickly as they flared, he snuffed them out. And drew up the memory of his mother's face as she'd looked just before she'd passed.

Pale. Waxen. Exhausted from the constant coughing and wheezing. Swollen from fluid buildup. Undiagnosed congenital heart failure had exacted a toll on her physically and emotionally. With regular doctor visits, proper medication and changes to her lifestyle, she could've managed the disease and enjoyed a longer life. But with mostly menial or low-paying jobs that offered no insurance for doctor appointments or prescriptions and being too busy working sometimes two jobs, she had been more concerned with providing shelter and food for him rather than focusing on herself. By the time Nico could afford to take care of her and convince her to go see about her health, it'd been too late. The disease had progressed.

A simple check to ease his mother's burden all those years could've made a drastic difference. But Barron, angry that she'd refused to abort Nico, had punished her. And Rhoda Morgan had been too proud to beg him to be in their lives. Not that it would've changed anything. By the time Nico was born, Barron had already become engaged to another woman. His replacement family had been in the works, and Barron had no need of Rhoda or his son. So he'd abandoned them, resigning them to a life of backbreaking work, struggle and poverty.

So yes. Fuck guilt and shame.

He'd lost the person he loved most in this world.

His rock. It was only fitting that he'd take the same from Barron since it'd been his negligence, arrogance and lack of humanity that set them on this path. Death didn't mean a damn thing. Nico's brand of hate exceeded the grave.

"Good," he finally replied to her as the town car pulled up in front of the department store's entrance. "Your brother and the bakery are depending on it."

Not waiting for his driver to open his door, Nico pushed it open and stepped out. Resolve and purpose settled on his shoulders, and he turned back toward the car, extending a hand toward her. She slipped her palm across his, and his fingers closed around hers, the large diamond pressing into flesh. As soon as she exited the vehicle, she didn't move forward but remained standing between him and the open car door. Tilting her head back, a smile curved her mouth, probably for the press that congregated on the sidewalk and the cameras that flashed and popped in their direction.

A consummate actress.

Oh, he knew just how good.

"Don't you dare threaten me," she snapped through a lovely smile and gritted teeth.

"Not a threat, baby girl," he murmured. To the observers outside the department store and to the reporters, it would appear as if he bent his head to whisper something sweet or flirtatious in her ear. "Just a reminder. Or motivation. Take it any way you want."

Lifting his head and stepping back, he held his arm out to her, and she settled her hand on the crook of his elbow. The small touch, though obligatory, burned through his tuxedo jacket and arrowed straight to his cock.

The jolt of lust grounded him, driving home the need to concentrate on the evening ahead and the ultimate goal. If he allowed the grinding arousal she stirred to distract him, he could lose everything.

She'd damn near eviscerated him once before.

Never again. This time, he was in control. Of the narrative, of his response to her and of their "relationship." And most importantly, when it ended.

Because when these three months were over, so were they. He would return to his life of the past three years—one where he depended only on himself. One that might be solitary but was also free of pain and betrayal. Free of her.

Just the way he preferred it.

Five

For the year and a half she'd been with Nico, Athena had moved in the more rarified circles of Boston society. The numerous fundraiser galas, dinner parties, gallery openings, business functions… They'd introduced her to a glittering, moneyed and privileged world she'd previously only read about in the gossip columns or come across online.

She hadn't missed it.

And now, temporarily back in the realm Nico navigated with a grace that belied his humbler upbringings, she wished to be anywhere else. Bromberg's department store had been closed to the public for tonight. The lower level and food court were transformed into a space worthy of a reception at the Met. Long gold and cream curtains hid the various food kiosks. Tiny gold lights wrapped around the columns soaring up to the fourth level, flowers intermingled with them, gifting the usually overbright area with an ethereal decor. High round tables draped in champagne-colored cloths dotted the floor, while chairs upholstered in the same soft color offered places to sit. A full bar had been erected on one side of the food court and a tuxedoed band currently played classical renditions of current Top 50 hits.

Among it all mingled the rich and connected of Boston's elite.

And then there was her.

"Can't make a silk purse out of a sow's ear, big sister. Isn't that what Mama always says?"

Her brother's voice sidled into her head, and for a second, she almost glanced around to see if he'd somehow sneaked his way into this gathering. Ridiculous. She gave her head a small shake, then stared down into her glass of champagne before finishing it off. That smug gem had come from Randall just after she and Nico had broken up. Her older brother's idea of consoling her had been to remind Athena she'd had no place in Nico's world in the first place. Not the first time he'd hinted at that during her relationship with Nico, but that last time had seared her soul.

Because when she'd walked out after he'd issued that final ultimatum—*if you move out of here to return to your parents' house, don't bother coming back*—Nico hadn't attempted to contact her. To try and save what they had. She'd been disposable and easily forgotten. And Randall's thoughtless words had only cemented what she'd already believed.

She didn't belong here. And maybe Nico never thought she did either.

Yet he was the one who'd dragged her back in. *For his reasons, his plans, not because he missed or needed you.*

Best she remember and keep that uppermost in her mind. Last time, it'd taken over a year to obtain any sense of her old self. If she dared to forget, she might find the road to recovery longer...or endless.

"Oh I don't know what caused that look on your face, but more champagne definitely cannot hurt the situation."

Before Athena could register that another person had not only joined her but had directed that pitying statement toward her, the empty glass she held disappeared. In seconds, a full glass replaced it. Glancing up from the golden, bubbly wine, Athena met a pair of dark brown eyes that reflected the smile curving her full mouth. The gorgeous, petite and curvy woman with natural dark curls that grazed her shoulders sipped from her own nearly full glass and eyed Athena over the rim.

"Sorry," the woman said, lifting a bare shoulder. "But you reminded me of *me* so much that I had to come over and introduce myself."

Athena made a show of scanning the crowd before returning her attention to the woman in front of her. "Black?"

The woman snickered. "Yes, that, too. I hate to say it, but it's true that when we spot the few Black people in the room, we gravitate toward them like they're long-lost family." She arched an eyebrow. "And pray they're not assholes."

Athena nodded but said nothing. Experience from years ago had taught her that people who approached and seemed friendly often did so with their own agenda on their minds, not a budding friendship. But her reticence didn't seem to discourage the woman in front of her.

"Smart." She lifted her glass in a small toast. "You don't know me. I could be coming over here, talking smack just to lure you into a false sense of security and then carry tales about how you trashed people in the room." She arched an eyebrow. "You might look like you'd rather be anywhere but here, but you've obviously been in these circles long enough. I'm still learning that pretty faces can sometimes hide the bitchiest of souls. And that is not gender specific."

Against her better judgment, Athena snorted. Because, *truth*. But the wealthy did not corner the market on trashy people. That trait transcended tax brackets.

"Eve Burke." The woman extended her hand toward Athena. "It's a pleasure to meet you…?"

"Athena Evans." She shook Eve's hand, her mind whirling.

Eve Burke. Kenan Rhodes's fiancée. And apparently the owner of Intimate Curves, the exclusive lingerie boutique that the guests in attendance would glimpse for the first time this evening. The unveiling of the brick-and-mortar version of what had previously been exclusively an online business—and a hugely successful one, at that—was the main reason for the party tonight. Nico had explained all of this after they'd initially arrived and had drinks and appetizers in hand.

Shit.

What had Eve said? Athena looked like she didn't want to be there. She was already messing up her one job. Heart thumping against her rib cage, Athena flipped through things to say to Nico's half brother's fiancée. Apologize? Offer an excuse? Or worse, another lie about how she was delighted to be here at Bromberg's?

No. Dammit, just…no. She couldn't add one more lie on top of the others. The biggest deception being the one weighing down her ring finger.

Yeah, not thinking about that right now.

What had Nico said? Better to stick as close to the truth as possible?

"To be honest," Athena said, silently ordering herself not to flinch, "I'm not at all comfortable in these settings." Leaning closer, she lowered her voice a shade and admitted, "I never know what to talk about. Somehow I doubt most of the people here care about how long you have to refrigerate crème brûlée before serving." She shrugged a shoulder. "So I end up standing there and smiling like an idiot. An idiot with a sore face at the end of the night."

"Oh my God, I think I might be crushing on you right now," Eve whispered, eyes gleaming with humor. "That's the most fascinating thing I've heard all night."

Athena laughed, and Eve grinned back at her.

"So you bake? Are you a chef? A caterer?" Eve asked, propping an elbow on the table next to them. "Real talk? I know nothing about cooking, especially baking. But I love to eat. As all these pretty curves attest to." She waved a hand down her divine, hourglass figure displayed to perfection in a floor-length, blush-colored bandage dress.

"My family owns Evans Bakery in Brighton."

"Did I hear Evans Bakery?" A woman with beautiful, long caramel hair and bright green eyes joined them. Clad in a royal blue, mermaid-style dress that highlighted her lush curves as well as her small baby bump, she reminded Athena of a Mother Earth pinup model. If such a thing existed. "When I first moved to Boston, I used to haunt that place. It had the most delicious snickerdoodles."

Pleasure flooded Athena for the first time since arriving. "My grandmother made those fresh every morning. They were her own recipe and she insisted on baking them herself. She wouldn't trust anyone outside the family with the recipe."

The other woman laughed. "I don't blame her. They were fabulous. I remember your grandmother. Petite woman, but a deep voice that carried over the whole bakery? Gray hair and brown eyes? And she wore an embroidered, dark red apron every time I went there."

Athena nodded, a bit of her pleasure snuffed out by an unexpected pinch of sorrow. "That was her. My grandfather gave her that apron, and she never worked without it."

"Was her," the woman softly repeated. Surprise ricocheted through Athena when the woman reached out, gripped her hand and squeezed. "I'm sorry. She treated me with kindness and never like a stranger. That meant the world to a young woman new to the city and without friends."

"Thank you," Athena rasped.

Oh God. Don't let her start tearing up in the middle of this event.

"Eve, who did you loose Devon on now? You know her sensitivity superpowers have only increased with pregnancy. Now she's about to have this poor woman weeping in her glass. And that's a perfectly good waste of champagne. That's the true crime here."

Devon Cole, well, Farrell now—Cain's wife. So the new woman who joined their group must be Mycah Farrell, and the big, brooding giant behind her wearing the impeccable black suit and long-suffering expression had to be Achilles. Nico's brother.

Curiosity swept through Athena at her first glimpse of one of his younger half siblings. Although as tall as Nico, that's where the similarities between the men ended. Achilles's long, thick black hair tied back into a bun and his warm brown skin declared a biracial heritage, and he carried more bulk than Nico. Then there were the startling blue-gray eyes that scanned over the group, and Athena quelled the urge to glance away when his gaze landed on her.

There.

There lay the resemblance. That incisive, intense gaze and the sharp intelligence behind it. She bet this man missed nothing, just like his unknown older brother.

"No, the true crime is I can't have the champagne," Devon muttered, but her soft smile and the hand that curved around her stomach contradicted the petulance in her statement. "If I can't have it, then everyone will drink a river of salty tears." Then she emitted a wicked cackle.

A bark of laughter broke free from Athena without her permission, and she covered her lips with a hand, but none of the others seemed to find her outburst inappropriate. No, they joined in. Even Achilles smiled.

"Since I now don't remember what it feels like *not* to be pregnant, I have zero sympathy. The taste of anything alcoholic is nothing but a distant memory to me." Mycah released an exaggerated, heavy sigh. With her large baby bump, the woman did appear to be on the verge of going into labor at any second. Yet, even with her lamentations about wine deprivation, happiness and...contentment sparkled in her dark eyes. Especially when she tilted her head back and pinned her husband with a look. "Your turn next time."

"Duly noted," Achilles said, solemnly nodding. Then he turned that aquamarine gaze on Athena. "And you are?"

Mycah swatted his arm, and he slid her a look that on another person would've clearly said, "What'd I say?" But on Achilles Farrell, it was the visual equivalent of a shrug.

"Please excuse him," Mycah said to Athena, then offered her a slim hand. "I'm Mycah Farrell and this bastion of manners and decorum is my husband, Achilles."

"It's a pleasure to meet you both." She accepted Mycah's hand and shook it, giving Achilles a nod. "I'm Athena Evans. I'm here with my fiancé, Nico Morgan." She'd managed to say *fiancé* without tripping over it. Go her.

Achilles's eyebrows drew down in a slight frown, but before she had time to wonder—okay, panic—over that, all three women turned in the direction where she'd left Nico. And stared.

"Wow," Devon whispered.

"That man has always been—*whew*," Mycah muttered. Then she patted Achilles's hand. "Not you 'whew,' though."

"Thanks," came his dry reply.

"I remember meeting him a couple of months ago at the board meeting to approve the Bromberg's renovation. He's one intense man." Eve tapped her bottom lip. "Intense is sexy."

"I'm sure she's talking about you," a new, masculine voice drawled.

Athena glanced over her shoulder to find two men, both tall and wide shouldered, but one white with dark, short hair and the other with light brown skin, close cut hair and clean-shaven. Both shared the same stunning eyes as Achilles, and it declared their identity to Athena.

Cain Farrell and Kenan Rhodes.

Without even trying, she'd found herself surrounded by Nico's family. The family he refused to acknowledge and didn't want anything to do with. Sadness sank inside her like a leaden ball. He was alone; with Rhoda's passing he had no one. And here stood six people who could be family for him, but Nico wouldn't allow it. It seemed he almost preferred a solitary existence marked only by business associations and shallow social attachments.

She gave her head a mental shake. Three years he'd been out of her life. She was the last one to presume anything about him.

Yet... The ache refused to subside.

Kenan waved his brother off. "Of course, she's talking about me. Who else would she describe as intense, sexy and gorgeous?"

"I must've blacked out for a moment, because I don't remember Eve saying *gorgeous*," Cain said, voice dry.

"I've been telling Devon to get that checked out. All the stress of impending fatherhood has probably affected your faculties. Because she definitely said *gorgeous*."

"Oh my God," Achilles growled.

A chuckle bubbled up Athena's throat, and maybe she didn't contain her amusement as well as she believed, because she drew the attention of all three men.

"Athena, these are my brothers Cain Farrell and Kenan Rhodes." Achilles introduced her. "Cain, Kenan, this is Athena Evans, Nico Morgan's fiancée."

"It's wonderful to meet you, Athena," Cain said, briefly but warmly clasping her hand in his. Kenan followed suit, smiling down at her. "And congratulations. I have to make sure and congratulate Nico as well."

"Now is as good a time as any," Nico said, materializing beside her and wrapping a strong arm around her waist.

An electric charge rippled through her, and she stiffened in reaction. It wasn't lost on her that the first time they'd truly touched after a three-year absence was an act for the benefit of an audience. It played with her head. While her brain screamed "This isn't right!" her sex cheered, "More, more, more!" It was laughable how much of a cliché she'd become.

As quick as she'd gone rigid, in the next moment, she deliberately relaxed against him, curving into his side. As she used to do. Her whole body...sighed. As if in relief or contentment. Because how many times had she dreamed of being held by him? Of having carte blanche to touch him? Even if it was under these circumstances...

But what if these were the perfect circumstances? What if she could indulge in touching him, and being touched by him, if just for these stolen moments? It would be harmless, a performance. It would be safe. And Nico would never know that she privately craved each caress, each embrace, each soft and hungry look and word.

It would be her little secret.

Cain shook Nico's hand, slapping him on the shoulder. "Congratulations, Nico." He grinned. "I need to take lessons from you on how to keep a relationship out of the press. I bet it's much less stressful that way."

Nico dipped his head and his hand stroked the curve of Athena's hip, leaving waves of heat behind. Swallowing a whimper, she took a sip from her glass, but the champagne did nothing to quench the fire.

"I don't think there's anything 'less stressful' about being with me," Nico said, voice heavy with self-deprecation. "And yet, Athena's stayed anyway."

"I told him, I'm adding my halo to our wedding gift registry," she drawled.

As Cain and Kenan laughed, she absorbed the small jolt that shivered through Nico. Surprise? Probably. Up until this moment, he had cause to be concerned about her acting skills. She hadn't been pulling her weight. But being weighed down with worries about not fucking up and lust for her costar kind of disrupted her focus.

"If that's the case, request a few more. We're in arrears with ours." Kenan grinned as Eve curled against him, wrapping her arms around his waist.

"You're right about that. I'm a saint and it's about time you recognize it." Eve smiled at Nico. "It's nice to see you again, Mr. Morgan. And thank you for coming out tonight and bringing Athena with you. I think it's only fair you should know that we're officially in a custody battle for her."

Nico arched an eyebrow, glancing down at Athena then at Eve. "Please, it's Nico. And I'll give you visitation but I'm going to have to insist on primary physical custody."

"Fine," she grumbled, eyes gleaming with humor.

"Cain, Athena runs Evans Bakery." Devon looped her arm through her husband's. "Remember I told you about the bakery I found after moving to Boston? And how it was one of the places that made me feel at home for the first time? That was Evans Bakery."

"That's a small world," Cain murmured, and when he looked at Athena again, she resisted the urge to lift her fingers to her face and check for any droplets of champagne. Did all the Farrell men own those scalpel-sharp stares? "So you own Evans?"

"My family does," she corrected, and though she didn't glance at Nico, displeasure damn near emanated from him. Anger flickered in her chest. *Yes, dammit. I know how you feel about my family. You've expressed it. Ad nauseum.* But because they were supposed to be a happy couple, she bit back the scorching retort. "You can usually find me there most days, though."

"How did you two meet?" Mycah asked. "The billionaire and the baker sounds like a really cute Hallmark movie or the start to a bad joke."

Athena snorted, and the corner of Nico's mouth quirked. "I think we're a little bit of both."

"And to answer your question, he squashed my buns." Six pairs of eyes landed on her, and she shrugged. "It's true."

"Okay, that's a story," Kenan said. "Gimmee." Then he arched an eyebrow and shook his head. "Nico, I feel like you should prepare to lose cool points. No worries. We won't judge you…too much."

"My grandmother had a longtime customer, and every birthday she'd make hot cross buns just for her. This year, Mrs. Lemmons had fallen ill and hadn't been to the bakery in weeks. Even though my grandmother passed, I still baked the hot cross buns for her and was going to deliver them. I'd just found a rare open parking spot in her Back Bay neighborhood and was heading toward her building when someone—" she tipped her head back and gave that "someone" a narrow-eyed mock glare "—came barreling out of nowhere and slammed right into me, crushing my buns between us."

"In my defense…" Nico began amid all the hoots of laughter. He held up a hand, palm out. "I was late for a lunch meeting for a charity function. This, by the way, did not impress Athena. I think 'rich boy,' 'eyes in your ass' and 'jacked up my buns' were tossed around, and she might've given me the finger."

"I did not!" Athena objected, tapping him on his tight abdomen.

Even caught up in the memory and onetime happiness of their real first meeting—albeit an altered version as she'd been on a delivery errand for her grandmother and he'd been on his way to a lunch date with his mother—she couldn't erase the feel of those firm muscles and warm skin from her hand. The feel of him was branded into her fingers. She barely resisted the urge to scrub her fingers down the side of her thigh.

"She did."

"So love at first sight, then?" Eve asked, grinning.

"For me?" Nico lifted a shoulder. "Yes. But her? Not so much. I had to track her down, apologize profusely, carry more buns to Mrs. Lemmons, drink the most god-awful tea in the world with her and then buy my weight in baked goods for the office. All that before she even agreed to let me take her on our first date."

"She was worth it, though," Achilles rumbled.

Nico leaned down and brushed his lips over her fore-head, and God help her, she closed her eyes, savoring the sweetness of it. The artificial sweetness.

"Every hot cross bun and swallow of tea that tasted like minty dirt," he murmured.

Achilles snorted, and a bark of laughter escaped her. The others' joined in, and Athena met Nico's dark gaze.

What a phenomenal actor.

Because for a moment, she almost believed the glim-mer of affection in his eyes and the warmth in his deep voice were real. But she knew better.

And all the pretending in the world wouldn't change reality.

Turning back to his family surrounding them, she resumed the performance.

"I think that went well," Athena said into the silence that filled the back of Nico's town car.

That silence carried weight, had density. And it

sat on her chest like a suffocating winter blanket. She longed to kick it off, free herself. Even if it was with inane conversation.

"It did. Better than I expected." He drummed his fingers on his thigh, staring out the side window.

More silence. More…heaviness.

"I liked them." His shoulders stiffened, but he didn't remove his gaze from the window or acknowledge her statement. "Your brothers and their wives and fiancée," she expounded. "They were very nice and not at all what I anticipated."

More silence.

"Your brothers… They seemed to like you. Definitely respect you." She studied his strong, chiseled profile and didn't miss the tensing of his jaw. "Are you sure—"

"Did you notice their eyes?" he murmured, his tone almost casual. "Farrell eyes. It's a family trait. Barron had them and he passed them down to his sons." He finally turned to look at her, and in the deep shadows, his dark eyes appeared more shadowed. "All of his sons except me."

Her breath stuttered, then stalled in her lungs, a looming sense of unease yawning wide in her belly. A part of her almost told him to stop, that she'd mind her business and leave the topic alone. But the other, bigger part hunkered down, hungry to discover anything else about him. The pieces of him that he'd hoarded when they'd been together. Yes, he'd shared with her more than he'd shared with anyone else outside his mother, but still, he'd held back, guarding himself.

From her.

It'd only deepened her craving for him, and not just physically, but emotionally. Back then, Nico had showered her with jewelry, clothes, fancy dinners, even a car. But she would've given up every last gift just to have his heart. And that hadn't been an option.

So now, three years later, here she was, still aching for…pieces.

"Where most men would be proud over the birth of their first child, his first words to my mom were, 'He doesn't have the Farrell eyes. This boy isn't mine.' And he followed those up with a paternity test. Do you know when Mom told me that story, she seemed embarrassed, ashamed? As if it were her fault he rejected me instead of his arrogance. She blamed herself for giving me her eyes." His mouth twisted in a corrupted semblance of a smile. "That one and only meeting with Barron I told you about? He bragged about that paternity test, and said though I didn't inherit his eyes, I did get his killer instinct when it came to business. Those fucking Farrell eyes. As a kid, I would've traded my soul for them. But as I grew older, I was thankful for my own. And not just because I didn't want to look in the mirror and see him. But now, not having the same color eyes as Barron's sons has allowed me to have business dealings with them without suspicion or questions regarding my identity. Irony, right?"

Fury mingled with a soul-deep grief. Fury at a dead man and grief for the damage he'd inflicted and left behind. What kind of man purposefully hurt others for his own sport? Especially his sons? No wonder Nico hated Barron Farrell. Yet…

Yet at what cost?

He'd already cut off a part of himself from the world, from other people. From her when they'd been together.

What price would this plan of his demand? Worry spiked inside her, and though an ocean of pain and anger lay between them, she still feared for him.

Feared he traveled the road to becoming a replica of his father.

"I'm sorry, Nico," she whispered.

"For what?" He shifted in his seat, more fully facing her. "For having a mother who was both parents to me? For discovering my biological father wasn't just an absentee sperm donor but a bastard? For allowing his neglect and spite to strengthen me?" He cocked his head. "Or for pressing an issue I told you to let go?"

"Yes…and no," she said, not flinching from his hooded stare. "Yes, I'm sorry for all of that, but mostly because no child should be rejected by the person who is supposed to love them unconditionally. We tell ourselves that doesn't leave a scar, but we're deceiving ourselves. And no matter how successful, wealthy, strong or powerful we become, it doesn't rewrite history or erase the pain. I'm sorry you have to know that."

"*We* tell ourselves? You know it, too, don't you, Athena?"

An old, familiar ache pulsed just under her rib cage. "Yes."

Leave it. Don't say anything else. Let. It. Go.

But her lips parted, and as if an invisible force drew the words out, they unraveled between them. "I've never sought out my biological parents. Do you know why?" She didn't give him time to answer because the words tumbled out. "Fear. And not just because I'm afraid of discovering the truth behind why they gave me up. But also, I'm terrified if Mom and Dad found out I wanted to search out my birth parents, they would be hurt and angry—and throw me away. How pathetic is that? Thirty years old and scared of being abandoned by her adoptive parents because I've already lost the ones I don't remember. The ones who rejected me when they gave me away."

"Athena, you don't—"

"I don't know their reasons. Yes, I get that here." She tapped her temple. "But here—" she splayed her fingers over her chest, her heart "—here, sometimes I just wonder what about me made it okay for them to hand me over to strangers." She let loose a raw chuckle and clasped her fingers in front of her, dropping her hands to her lap. Staring down at them, she shook her head. "God, that sounds incredibly self-pitying and ungrateful. Those strangers ended up being absolutely wonderful parents. I shouldn't complain—"

"You're entitled to your feelings, baby girl. And you should never apologize for them."

His "baby girl" slid through her like thick molasses on a Sunday morning. Warmth filled her, offering her something sweet and sinful. It wasn't the first time he'd said the sexy endearment. With barely a tug on her imagination, memories of other times he'd uttered it wavered in her head. Whispering it against her lips before he took her in a searing kiss. Groaning it into her ear as he pushed deep, so damn deep inside her. Breathing it against her damp neck as his big body shuddered above her.

"And you?" she asked.

"What about me?"

Caution. The warning snapped like a red flag in a winter wind. But she couldn't heed it. Not when the dimness of the car's interior and the privacy glass encased them in their own private world. Not when recklessness bubbled inside her. So she pushed, even knowing he could very well lash out.

"You were hurt. *Barron* hurt you. And that's the purpose behind this plan, isn't it? To hurt him back?"

He didn't move, but she *felt* his emotional withdrawal.

"The performance ended as soon as we left the department store. Don't try and pretend to know me, Athena."

Oh she should've remembered that when he did lash out, it wasn't hot and quick. Nico turned cold, his cuts like freezer burn.

"I wouldn't dare claim to know you," she said, voice low, but by some minor miracle, steady. "Even after moving in with you, sharing your bed and loving you, I still wouldn't say it."

"Loving me?" The corner of his mouth curved, and he softly chuckled, the sound ugly, dark. "Is that what you called it? Did you love me when you walked out and didn't look back? If that's love—" he sneered the word as if it left a filthy taste in his mouth "—then I want no part of it. Love is fickle, faithless and will betray you as soon as look at you."

"Yes," she admitted. "I loved you even when I left. I loved you so much that it was a matter of survival. Stay in a relationship knowing you were only willing to give me pieces of you while I gave you all of me. Or leave, choosing more for myself."

"You never offered me the chance to give you more. You never asked."

"Every time I said 'I love you,' I asked," she murmured.

His head jerked back as if she'd clipped him in the chin. An emotion passed over his face, there and gone before she could decipher it in the shadows.

"Don't twist this around," he ground out, slashing a hand through the air. "You left because your family called and you came running like you always did. And nothing's changed. Before you take my inventory, you need to start taking account of your own. If it makes you feel better to blame me, go ahead, but we both know I, or any man, will never be able to compete with the only loyalty and love you have."

"You wanted me to cut them off," she hotly objected, slamming a hand up, palm out. "You're right. I won't do that."

"No, Athena." He leaned back, his expression shuddered, eyes opaque. "That's what you never understood. I didn't want you to cut them off. I just needed you to make room for me, too."

I just needed you to make room for me, too.

The statement rebounded off her skull but resonated in her heart.

That's not true!

The objection surged up her throat, hovering on her tongue. Her family had needed—still needed—her in a way he hadn't. Toward the end of their relationship, she'd been a silent roommate and lover. He'd spoken of irony.

No, the greatest irony was he needed her now, to infiltrate his half brothers' inner circle, in a way he never had needed her when they'd been together.

So if it'd seemed like she put her family first, maybe it'd been because they'd done the same with her.

Did they, though? Or did they take advantage of your willingness to always be there?

She shook her head as if it could dislodge that disloyal thought.

But Nico continued in the same flat tone, "But that was then, and we're not back there. We'll never go back there." The car pulled to a stop in front of her condo, and he pushed open the door, stepping outside. He turned to her, extending his hand. By rote, she slid her palm across his and allowed him to guide her out of the vehicle. As soon as she cleared it, he dropped her hand and shifted backward. It was a small movement, but huge. Loud. "We made our choices. That's the past, and from now on, let's focus on the present. Keep your end of the bargain, and I'll keep mine. Then we can part ways—again."

He didn't add "for good," but it echoed on the warm night air.

Silly her for trying to breach those carefully constructed, barbed wire fences that guarded his feelings, his heart. She should've remembered the consequences of trying to scale those walls. Last time, she'd survived with a shattered heart. If she dared to forget, the damage would be much worse a second time.

But she wouldn't forget again.

No, he'd reminded her clearly of the lesson she'd learned three years ago.

Nico Morgan broke things and didn't stick around to piece them back together.

Six

"Hey, big sister. You're looking awfully comfortable there behind my desk."

Gritting her teeth, Athena looked up from the payroll system to see her brother leaning a shoulder against the bakery office door, grinning.

That grin contained charm and humor. But his emphasis on "my desk" kind of peeled away some of that charisma. Randall seemed to enjoy getting in subtle digs and reminding her that he owned the bakery, and she was no more than an employee.

Usually, she ignored his immature need to assert his dominance. Today, though, she wasn't in the mood.

She'd asked—no, demanded—one thing of her mother before she agreed to the bargain with Nico. Get Randall into the bakery to take over the managerial duties she'd assumed in his absence. In the last three weeks, she'd attended more social events than she had in the last three years. Nearly every night, she accompanied Nico to dinners and parties in his bid to appear more approachable and—how had he put it?— *human* to his half brothers. And nearly every night, she'd returned home stressed, emotionally drained and so turned on. Touching herself to thoughts of him had become a nightly routine, like brushing her teeth.

Shower. Floss. Orgasm. Repeat.

Needless to say, early four o'clock mornings at the bakery were a thing of the recent past. And yes, she could've gone into the store later in the morning or afternoon. But she'd refused, granting Randall the chance to step up and prove himself a responsible leader. And son and brother.

The call she'd received last night from one of the employees disabused her of that idea.

Payroll had been missed last week. They'd asked Kira about their wages, and her sister had promised to let Randall know, but he hadn't shown up to the bakery, and the bakery's employees had gone without a paycheck. Why Kira hadn't called her...

God, Athena had to stop deluding herself. She knew perfectly well why her sister hadn't reached out to her. Their mother had probably forbidden it. Because then Athena would know Randall had been...being Randall.

Frustration coalesced inside her. Frustration threaded with resentment.

Frustration because her mother would rather not pay their loyal, hardworking employees than order her son to *do. His. Fucking. Job.*

Resentment because her parents, fully aware their

son was an overgrown boy who hadn't shown the slightest interest in the bakery while Mama was alive, had still turned the reins over to him. Because he had a penis.

No, because he was a *real* Evans.

Yet they expected the oldest, passed over child with the unknown bloodline to helm the ship. To smile, accept the dismissal of her tireless hours and faithful commitment and carry on as usual.

A live coal burned in her belly, and it had bitterness branded into it. When had she become so cynical, so unsatisfied, so…angry? Staring at her brother as he straightened, stretched and sauntered into the tiny office, a king surveying his land, that piece of coal burned red.

Handsome, with tawny skin and dark brown eyes, Randall had always been popular. Whether it'd been school, sports or just in the neighborhood, he was known for his playful, outgoing, always-up-for-a-good-time demeanor. And he hadn't been required to grow up. Randall Evans, the Peter Pan of Dorchester.

Even now, he ambled in wearing clothes wrinkled to hell and back, giving her the impression he was just rolling in from a long night out.

Wow.

"I will move and let you finish up payroll. Just say the word," Athena said, smiling and holding up her hands. "Is that why you're here today? To take care of it?"

His grin didn't waver, but his eyes narrowed. Right. Because they both knew that was not the reason he'd decided to show up. The true reason remained unclear, but she'd bet her brother hadn't suddenly appeared to work.

"No." Randall waved a hand at her, and she ground her teeth at the entitled gesture. "You got it. Besides, that's what you do. I trust you to handle it."

Handle it? She'd been *handling it* since Mama's stroke almost three years ago. *Her.* Their parents hadn't been involved in the business in years, and when their grandmother became ill, Athena had stepped up. So yes, *handling it* was her forte.

"Well, I hope you remember the training we received on the system. Because I'm going to be unavailable to do this again for the next few months. The only reason I'm in today is because our employees have gone a week without pay."

"*My* employees should've called me instead of you if there was an issue."

She snorted, and Randall lost his grin.

"You have something to say?" he asked, voice low.

"Yes." She tilted her head, studied him. The faintly red eyes, the sullen curve of his mouth. All signs of spoiled behavior. "If Kira could've called you, she would have. If the employees knew you or your number in the first place, they might have contacted you. But should've-could've doesn't pay the bills or their wages."

"I'm the owner of this bakery, big sister. Mom and Dad decided I should take it over, not you. That means you work for me, and if I need you to take care of the payroll, then you'll do it without all the lip."

"Wrong." Fury vibrated through her, and she rose from her chair. "I don't work for you. You don't pay me a salary. I've taken over this bakery because you've been an absentee boss. I've done this family a favor by stepping into the hole you've left. But don't ever get it twisted, Randall. You didn't hire me, and you can't give me orders. You never have and don't think you can start today."

He smirked. "And yet, here you are. Taking care of business. Keeping the place running."

"Not for you."

"Same difference." He shrugged. "But whatever. If you don't want to do it anymore, show Kira. She can take over payroll. I don't know what the hell crawled up your ass."

Ten. Nine. Eight. Seven... She counted down, dragging in breaths.

You can't put hands on him. One, he's your brother. And two, you won't do well in jail.

"What're you doing here?" she finally asked.

"Do I need a reason?" he scoffed. When he hadn't been here in years? Why yes, he did need a reason. "But Mom called and asked me to come over and check on things."

Athena bit the inside of her cheek, swallowing down a flaming retort. More likely, Mom told him to meet Athena here, claiming she had something to tell Randall. In other words, let Athena take care of the dirty work.

"Kira cannot take over the payroll since she doesn't know the system. If you don't remember, the number to the company representative is in the email contacts. She'll come out and give everyone a refresher training course. You'll need to do this ASAP since I won't be available for the next pay period." Leaning down, she tapped several keys and closed out of the program. "Last week is taken care of, and since you're here, you can cover the rest of the shift."

Athena pulled open the bottom drawer, removed her purse and then rounded the desk. Pausing in front of her brother, she tipped her head back and met his defiant dark gaze.

"So you're just abandoning the bakery? Leaving us high and dry?" he sneered. "Kira mentioned something about Nico Morgan showing up here a few weeks ago. That would explain this sudden switch in attitude. When you were with him years ago, before he dropped you like a bad habit, you acted all brand-new then, too."

She recoiled from his verbal attack, blinking up at him. "Are you serious right now?" she rasped. "You would say that to me when I've done nothing but show up every day for this place, for this family? For three years, since Mama had her stroke, since she died, where have you been? Even before that? The only thing you've done for this bakery, for this family is put us in more debt," she snapped. His chin jerked back toward his neck, and she nodded, emitting a harsh chuckle. "Oh yeah, Randall, I know about the three-hundred-thousand-dollar loan. And so does Mom, even though she won't say anything to you. So don't you dare come at me about what I'm doing for the bakery. We're not even on the same playing field."

"Y-you know about that? Mom does?" he stammered, swallowed. His eyes jumped over the office, as if their mother would suddenly appear from one of the corners. "How did you find out about that?"

"Does it matter?" She hiked the strap of her purse

over her shoulder. "What does matter is you didn't say anything about it to Mom or Dad and you haven't made a payment in months. When would any of us have found out? The day the authorities came to put chains on the bakery's doors?" She shook her head, not bothering to hide her disgust. "No, Randall, don't you come at me about abandoning Evans. You did when you put it up as collateral for a loan with no concern for the employment of anyone who worked here. And for what? What do you have to show for it? Maybe you can give our mother those answers."

"What did Mom say?" He shifted forward, grasping her upper arm. Panic laced his voice, and his eyes widened. "What're we going to do?"

The terms of her deal with Nico prevented her from divulging the truth to Randall. Of how she'd agreed to be Nico's fake girlfriend in order to cover his debt. But even if he hadn't issued that stipulation, Athena wouldn't have told Randall. He deserved to sweat over this dangerous decision that placed their business, their livelihood in jeopardy.

"We?" She arched an eyebrow. "We didn't take out that loan. You did. I don't know what your plans were to repay it at the time, but you should probably get on that."

His grip on her tightened, and he gave her arm a small shake. "What about your boy? You can't ask Nico Morgan for a small loan? Hell, he's a millionaire. A few hundred thousand is a drop in a bucket to him. He'll—"

"No." Her answer, flat, final, resonated in the room. "I will *not* ask him that. It's not his responsibility either. I don't care how many millions he has to spare."

Yes, Nico was prepared to pay the debt if she successfully held up her end of the bargain, but she hadn't *asked* for his help or his money. And she wouldn't sink that low, to use him for what she hadn't earned.

Randall's face twisted into a mask of rage. "You're such a holy roller." His hold on her hardened, and no doubt bruises would mar her skin. "Well, Athena, you're not. And when that asshole drops you again, you'll find out you're no better than the rest of us."

Yanking her arm free of his grasp and ignoring the throb, she shifted backward, out of his reach.

"Don't turn this on me," she said, pain at his ugly words an open wound inside her. She hitched up her chin. "Like I told Mom, this is your mess to clean up. And you can start by taking responsibility for *your* bakery. By showing up every day. By managing it." By showing he freaking cared.

"And where are you going to be? Too busy playing house with your millionaire boyfriend to help your family out?"

That stung. But his ungrateful, self-entitled attitude stung even more.

Giving him one last long look, she didn't bother dignifying his question with an answer. Instead, she moved past him and out the door, well aware she wasn't just leaving her brother in the office. She left the bakery in his hands. And that scared her.

All she could do was pray that by the time Nico paid off the bank loan, there would be a bakery left to save.

Seven

Nico knocked on Athena's apartment door, impatience whispering through him. He didn't need to pull his phone from his pocket to glimpse the time and see they had about forty minutes before the fundraiser ball benefiting pediatric medical research. Of all the social events they'd attended in the last few weeks, this one could be termed the social event of the season. With ticket prices ranging from fifteen to sixty thousand, a silent auction and games with prizes such as seats at New York Fashion Week or a walk-on role on a major motion picture, most of Boston's social and business elite attended. It was not only an opportunity to further his agenda with the Farrells, but the ball also presented other advantageous networking opportunities.

Now if only Athena would open the door.

He knocked again, unease joining the impatience.

Earlier, when he'd called to make sure she would be ready, Athena had sounded a little…off. Not distant as had been the case since their confrontation in the back of his town car after the Bromberg's reception. But definitely subdued.

His disquiet increased, and just as he raised his hand to rap on the door once more, it opened. Athena stood in the doorway.

Like every time he saw her, she struck him momentarily deaf and mute. Her beauty. Her innate sensuality that she wore more perfectly than the gorgeous lilac gown that molded to every curve of her tall, slender, deliciously curved body.

He deserved a fucking medal for keeping his hands to himself.

But he had, and not just because losing his focus would prove detrimental. The full, humiliating reason lay in him. He feared losing himself in her. Touching her, tasting her, becoming reacquainted with the wet, tight clasp of her body would be the slippery slope into a dangerous pit he might not be able to claw his way free of.

He'd slipped that night at the Bromberg's reception. Wrapping his arm around her waist, caressing her hip, inhaling her sweet scent, teasing her, laughing with her… For a moment, he'd forgotten it all was an act. For a moment, he'd allowed himself to sink into the fantasy. And when they'd left the reception, reality had been waiting. It'd doused him in a frigid wave.

Forgetting the pretense wasn't an option. Not if he wanted to emerge from this unscathed.

And he intended to do just that.

Skimming his gaze up her silk-clad body, he asked, "Are you—what's wrong?"

Not your damn business, he growled to himself. But as he narrowed his eyes on her, he didn't rescind the question. Question, hell. Demand.

Because there *was* something wrong. That disquiet that had curdled in his gut earlier returned. On the surface, Athena appeared as beautiful and composed as ever. But a closer inspection revealed the shadows that dimmed the vibrant green in her hazel eyes, the rigidness that invaded her usually graceful frame. The tightness around her lush mouth.

Small details that most people wouldn't notice. But he wasn't most people. He'd spent a year and half learning every inch of her face, body and demeanor. And three years remembering…everything.

"Athena," he said, stepping into her apartment. "What's wrong? And don't tell me nothing."

She snapped her lips shut and frowned up at him. For his high-handedness or moving into her home, he didn't know. Probably both, but she turned and walked inside, leaving Nico to close the front door behind him.

"Just give me a few minutes to grab my purse and put on my shoes, and I'll be ready," she said, avoiding his question.

As if it would be that easy.

"Athena." He called her name again, softer but no less firm. "We're not going anywhere until you answer my question."

She huffed out a breath, then halted midstride, whirling around to face him. With her mouth in a grim line, she glared at him. But as he prepared to dig in for an argument, her expression gentled—no, unraveled. She seemed to wilt before his eyes. Pinching the bridge of her nose, she closed her eyes.

"I'd rather not do this, Nico. Take my word for it, you don't want to have this conversation. So let me just finish getting ready so we can head out."

"No." Even as every instinct he possessed screamed to maintain his distance, he crossed the space separating them and circled her wrist, tugging her arm away from her face. "Look at me, Athena." He waited. And several seconds later, she complied, her thick fringe of lashes lifting. Those stunning hazel eyes met his, and a spiral of heat corkscrewed in his gut. "Talk to me, baby girl. What's wrong?"

"This is about my family. My brother. You still want to talk?"

She threw the information down like a gauntlet. And he smothered the flare of anger at the mention of Randall Evans. This wasn't about her brother, about the dysfunction that existed within her family.

This was about her.

Correction. If he couldn't get her to talk about what bothered her, then that would affect the performance he required of her. He needed her to be at her best, her sharpest. It benefited him to hear her out.

It wasn't personal.

Fuck, he could spin bullshit when needed.

"Yes, I want to talk."

She stared at him, as if weighing the veracity of his words. Her teeth sank into her bottom lip, one of her tells, and he curled his fingers into his palm, preventing himself from smoothing his thumb across that lip. From following the caress with one from his tongue.

Dragging his gaze from her mouth, he met her eyes again. And didn't miss the flash of heat there. That blaze stirred an answering one in him, tossing kindling on already simmering flames.

Blinking, she glanced away. "I'm sorry. It's been a… trying day. Seriously, though. I'm good—"

"Athena."

She sighed. "Fine. You're incredibly stubborn," she muttered. "I received a call from one of the bakery's employees last night. She, along with the others, hadn't been paid. My mother had agreed to get my brother more involved with the store, to cover me because I couldn't—wouldn't—work *and* pay his debt. Needless to say, that didn't happen. And our employees are paying for it—or are *not* getting paid for it." She heaved another sigh and smoothed her hands over the curls brushed into a bun at the nape of her neck. "I couldn't allow another day to go by without them getting a check, so I went into the bakery and Randall showed up. We got into it, and I told him I knew about the loan, although not about our—" she waved a hand back and forth between them "—arrangement. I left him sweating it out and not long after I left the bakery, my mom called me."

Damn. He didn't need the gift of clairvoyance to see where this was headed.

On bare feet, she strode toward her kitchen. Within moments, she returned with a bottle of wine and two glasses. She didn't ask if he wanted to partake but poured him some anyway. Sliding one of the elegant flutes toward him across the breakfast bar, she picked up the other and sipped. Only then did she continue.

Staring down into the deep red depths, she said, "Mom was not happy." She flicked a look at him. "She hasn't been happy with you since that NDA, but she's abided by it. Still, it's stuck in her craw, and since she can't take it out on you, I've been the lucky candidate." The corner of her mouth quirked, then she took another sip. "Randall had phoned her, of course, complaining. He doesn't want to be at the bakery because he has more important things to do, and why can't I just run it like I have been? And he'd only acquired the loan to invest the money so he could make improvements to the bakery. I called bullshit. Because if that were true, then why is this the first time we're hearing about it? But Mom bought it, hook, line and my-baby-wouldn't-lie-to-me. And now, because Randall is *so* busy—still don't know with what—she wants me to cover his loan *and* come back and run the bakery for him. All because he called and whined. As usual. Still no consequences for his actions."

"What did you tell her?" he asked, attempting to remain neutral.

She slowly lowered her glass to the breakfast bar and lifted her gaze to his. The shadows that swirled in her gaze couldn't conceal the turmoil and hurt there. And his grip on the glass tightened.

"I told her no," she quietly said. "Just because she's flipped the script and changed her mind doesn't mean I will. And she's furious." Her tremulous whisper belied the smile that ghosted across her lips. "She called me selfish. *Selfish*. I think she could've called me a bitch and it would've been less offensive, less hurtful. She told me to call her back when I've decided to put family ahead of my own petty grievances." Athena leaned her head back and laughed, the sound jagged…wounded. When she quieted, she looked at him, reaching for her glass of wine. "Go ahead, say it. Because as much as Mom never cared for you, the feeling was more than mutual. Here's your chance to say, 'I told you so.'"

Several blistering comments leaped to his tongue. About her lazy, manipulative brother. About how her family wouldn't know a boundary if it flashed its neon red tits. About how they didn't appreciate her, took advantage of her kindness…of her almost desperate need for their approval.

Oh yes, there was plenty he could say.

Instead, he went with, "What would you like for dinner?"

Athena froze, the glass midway between the bar and her mouth. Blinking, she peered at him. "I'm sorry?"

"Dinner. I'll have it delivered. You have a taste for something in particular?"

She frowned, once more setting the wine down. "I'm confused. What about the ball? We're not going?"

"No."

Shock melted into confusion and then into understanding. Well, at least that made one of them. Even though he'd said the words, part of him still couldn't believe it. Not twenty minutes ago, he'd been impatient to leave for the social event of the season, and now he was blowing it off.

"But why? I thought tonight was important," she murmured.

Because you're in no state to attend a gala.

Because you're hurting.

Because someone needs to put you first today.

"One ball is the same as another." He shrugged a shoulder. "Unless," he arched an eyebrow, "you're just dying to attend?"

She smiled, and it was only a curve at the corner of her mouth, but it contained genuine warmth. "Somehow I think I'll carry on if I miss this one."

"Good." He looked away from her, from the eyes that were a shade freer of shadows. "About dinner... I'm feeling Italian or Chinese. Is that good with you?"

"Either sounds perfect. And Nico?"

He looked up from pulling up a browser on his phone. "Yes?"

"Thank you."

"You're welcome." He cocked his head. "Now, lasagna or shrimp egg foo yong?"

"I'm not discussing this with you anymore."

"Hah!" Athena stabbed her tiramisu-stained fork in his direction, a triumphant grin stretched across her face. "That's the refrain of a loser."

"No, it's the statement of someone who refuses to argue with an illogical person," Nico shot back.

Athena chuckled, the sound wicked. "Illogical? When you start tossing insults, it's another sign you've been thoroughly beaten. Just admit it. You're wrong."

"I'm not."

"You *so* are."

Nico ground his teeth together. "We're going to have to agree to disagree. Although you're wrong as hell."

"Say it," she sang. "Just say it. Gandalf is a better wizard than Dumbledore."

"I don't know what's in that tiramisu," he said, jabbing a finger at the half-eaten dessert, "but no doubt it's one hundred proof."

Snickering, she scooped more of the sweet into her mouth and hummed in pleasure. He swallowed down a curse as his cock jerked behind the zipper of his tuxedo pants. His heart squeezed at the humor in her eyes, no traces of her earlier pain in evidence.

"You're still a sore loser, Nico."

"That would imply that you're the winner of this argument. And that would be a fallacy, Athena."

More chuckling, and Nico fought back a smile. Rising from the couch, he said, "I'm a little afraid to offer you more wine, but can I get you another glass?"

She grabbed hers off the coffee table and held it up with a wide grin. "Yes, please."

Shaking his head, he headed for the kitchen for refills of the Moscato. As he returned to the living room with the two glasses, he surveyed the open floor space of her condo, as he often did when he arrived to pick her up. The ordinariness of it struck him again. There was nothing wrong with the matching canisters in the kitchen or the landscape painting on the wall of the living room or the royal blue throw rug in the hallway. All perfectly fine—for an apartment staged by a real estate agent preparing for a showing.

Athena was missing.

"Why're you looking around like that?" Athena asked as he stepped down into the living room.

"Like what?" Nico handed her a glass and sank down onto the couch.

She tapped a finger against the bowl of her glass. "Like you're trying to figure out a puzzle."

"That's pretty accurate," he said, weighing whether he should go forward with the conversation.

They'd enjoyed a rare, good evening. One where the thorny past hadn't intruded. Even now, she sat, curled up on the sofa, dressed in a loose-fitting, off-the-shoulder T-shirt and black leggings. He'd shed his jacket and bow tie and had rolled his sleeves back. Since they'd reentered each other's lives, it was the most relaxed they'd been together. Almost as if they'd silently agreed to lower their guard. At least for tonight.

And he loathed fucking up that temporary truce.

"Let me guess what you're thinking right now," she murmured, leaning forward and cradling her wine. "We're having a great evening where no verbal swords have been crossed or blood shed, and you don't want to ruin it with a possible argument. Let me make you a promise." She held up a hand, palm out. "I hereby do solemnly swear not to be offended at whatever comes out of your mouth. Or not to show it."

He huffed out a soft laugh, and after a moment, nodded. Scanning her living room once more, he frowned.

"I'm assuming you moved to Cambridge to be closer to your grandmother, but what happened here? In this apartment," he clarified. "I remember your old place, and how you put your stamp on mine. Kitschy shit, refurbished pieces from flea markets, framed photographs or art from local artists. This—" he took another visual tour of the apartment, gestured toward the perfectly bland wooden-fruit-in-a-bowl centerpiece on the coffee table "—is almost sanitized. It's not you."

She didn't immediately answer but scanned the room as if seeing it for the first time. And maybe, in a sense, she was. Through his eyes.

"You're right. I did move here after Mama went into assisted living a couple of years ago. If I wasn't at the bakery, I spent my time there, only coming here to sleep and shower. And since she's passed, I just…" She again shrugged a shoulder. "I guess I just haven't viewed this place as anything more than a way station. It's hard to transition from that thinking to something else."

He frowned, tipping his head to the side. "Why were you so worried about your grandmother? Wasn't that part of the reason behind her moving to the facility? To ease your concern about her care? Cambridge Grounds is one of the best assisted living residences in the state."

"Yes, they were wonderful. That wasn't the problem— Wait. How do you know what facility she was at? I didn't mention the name, and we broke up before she went to Cambridge Grounds."

Shit.

He slowly leaned backward until the arm of the couch pressed into his spine. For two years, he'd kept his promise, maintained his silence. Not that it'd been hard. Though he had no use for most of her family, he'd always respected Glory Evans. Respected and liked her. It'd been Glory he'd visited and asked for her blessing before proposing to Athena, not her father. So, yes, he held the woman in high esteem and had intended on guarding their secret past her death. But then, he hadn't expected to become involved with Athena again either.

Just…*shit*.

"Nico?" Her gaze roamed his face as if seeking answers. And maybe she found them in his eyes or in his silence. Or more logically, her quick brain worked it out. She flattened her hands on either side of her hips, bracing herself. Against the truth? Maybe. "You. It was you," she breathed, a quick emotion spasming across her face. "Mama said a grant or some social service aid came through that paid for Cambridge Grounds. We didn't want her to leave home, but she insisted on going, especially since all the expenses were covered. At the time, I didn't question the story. Not even when I visited the facility. She had her own private room, the staff was professional and attentive, the building and grounds were immaculate. I was just happy she would be somewhere safe, clean and comfortable. Somewhere she seemed content. And she was. Right until…"

Athena trailed off, blinked. When she lifted her hazel eyes back to him, they contained bruised shadows, pain. Everything primal within him howled to haul her across his lap. To curl his body around hers and protect her from that hurt. But even if that was his right—which it wasn't—she didn't want that from him.

"Tell me the truth." Though softly spoken, she didn't issue the words as a request. No, it was pure, velvet demand. Yet, underneath, he caught the plea. The need.

He couldn't resist that need. To be honest, he never could.

"Yes, I paid for your grandmother's assisted living care."

Her low inhale echoed sharply in the room, and she

stared at him, the scrutiny bordering on invasive. But he didn't glance away.

"Why?" she rasped. "Why did you do it? We weren't together. We..."

"Because your grandmother asked me to."

Her head snapped back as if his blunt statement tapped her in the chin. "What? No, you're lying. Why would she do that? She knew about—"

"Yes, she knew how you felt about me. But she loved you. Worried about you. And that trumped your feelings over her reaching out to me." He worked his jaw, uneasy with betraying a confidence, even though Glory Evans was gone. But knowing the kind of woman she'd been, Nico didn't think she would mind so much now. Especially if it meant releasing Athena from whatever guilt held her captive. "Glory hated that you moved back into your parents' home after her stroke."

Athena's gasp broke on the air between them, and this time, he had no problem deciphering the emotion twisting her lovely features. Hurt. Sorrow.

He swore low and long under his breath. "Athena," he murmured, breaking his personal vow and extending his hand toward her.

But she recoiled, pressing back against the corner of the couch, shaking her head. "That's not true," she whispered. "I moved back to take care of her. Because I loved her. That's just not true."

Dammit.

He couldn't stand it. Fuck what had come between them before now. That agony in her voice. The hint of the lost, insecure girl so uncertain of love...

He stood, and in two short strides he curled his hands

underneath her arms and lifted Athena from the couch. In the next moment, he claimed her place and settled Athena on his thighs, wrapping his arms around her. Though he held her, a part of him braced for her rejection. They weren't in front of an audience; he had no legitimate reason to touch her. Other than every protective instinct when it came to this woman roaring that he do just that. So he waited for her to wiggle out of his embrace and demand to know what the hell he was doing.

But she didn't.

Instead she hid her face in his neck, her warm breath bathing the base of his throat. Her arms encircled his chest, and she curled against him, as if seeking his heat…his protection. That thought shouldn't cause a growl of satisfaction to rumble in his chest. Shouldn't have pleasure careening through him or his head bending to brush a kiss over the top of her head.

"She loved you," he said, his lips moving against her thick curls. "She loved all of her grandchildren, but she found a kindred spirit in you. And she wanted only the best for you—your happiness, your peace…your freedom. Which is why it saddened her when you moved back home. Because she hated being a burden on you."

"She could never be a burden." She fisted the back of his shirt. "Why would she think that? We're family. I would've done anything for her."

"She knew that, too. She also knew…" He hesitated, her family being a touchy subject between them. "She knew your family would place most of the responsibility for her care on your shoulders, and you would accept it because of your love for her. Glory couldn't do anything about it that first year, but as soon as she had some of her mobility and speech back, she contacted me. Your grandmother—" he shook his head, and a smile played about his mouth in remembrance of the strong, feisty woman "—she was proud. I was aware of her story, of how her and her husband had built their business from the ground up. It couldn't have been easy to come to me, a man she believed hurt her granddaughter. But she did. For you, she would've sacrificed anything. And understand this, Athena." He leaned back, lifting his hands between them to cup her face and tilt it back so she had no choice but to meet his eyes. Glimpse the truth there.

"Coming to me? Asking that I cover the assisted living expenses? Moving from the only home she'd known for decades? It was all for you. Because Glory knew if she didn't leave, you wouldn't either. And more than anything, she wanted you to have your independence, your freedom back."

A breath shuddered from between Athena's lips and her thick fringe of lashes fluttered down. But that didn't prevent a tear from tracking down her cheek.

Even though his brain blared a high-pitched warning, he bowed his head and rubbed the moisture away...with his lips. The saltiness hit his tongue, and he shifted to the other side, claiming another tear. Behind him, her hands balled his shirt tighter, harder, stretching the material across his back.

Lust left him intoxicated, off-balance. Burning up. Before he teetered over the edge and committed a sin they would both pay for, he raised his head, staring down into her flushed face. He shouldn't have touched her. Or kissed away her tears. No, he shouldn't have cradled her, hugged her, buried his nose in her hair, inhaled her sugar-and-vanilla scent. He'd crossed a line, and now he struggled to drag his ass back across it.

Because he'd done a lot of things in his life—some he was proud of, some not so much. But he couldn't take advantage of her vulnerability. That he refused to do.

Dropping his hands from her face, he murmured, "Athena."

She released his shirt and cuffed his wrists, holding on to him.

"She always liked you. Trusted you," she whispered. "In hindsight, I'm not surprised she went to you. I'm…" She swept her mouth over the heel of his palm, and electrical currents pulsed up his arm, down his spine. He ground his teeth against the charge, battled the need to take that delectable mouth with his own while spreading her legs and rocking his dick over her pretty sex. He ordered his body to stand down and focused on her soft admission. "I'm grateful she had you to turn to. Thank you for taking care of my grandmother, Nico."

He locked down the groan that barreled up his throat as she delivered another caress to his hand. Until that moment, the lines in his palm had just been that—creases. But now they'd transformed into erotic hot spots that connected straight to his cock. And it required every ounce of his control not to shake his hands free, burrow his fingers through her hair and drag her head back so he could suck the elegant column of her throat. Mark it. Bruise it, so when she looked in the mirror the next morning, she would feel him, never forget him.

Fuck, he needed space before he did something stupid that neither of them could take back.

Gently but firmly, he released his wrists and cradled

her head. Once more, he tipped her head back, ensuring she looked at him.

"You know who I am, Athena. What I am," he said, unable to keep the growl from his voice. "And right now, all I'm thinking about is if you'll open up wide and let me fuck this pretty mouth. Or if you'll make me work for it, starting with soft kisses, gentle bites."

He tipped her head back farther, lowering his until their breath mingled, mated. "But I'm not in the habit of taking advantage of women when they're in a vulnerable place. Next time you're on my lap, though, ass against my cock and lips against my skin, I won't hold back. Not until your nails are digging in my back and your voice is hoarse from screaming my name." He bent his head closer, eliminating all but a mere inch of space between them. "Not until this tight, gorgeous little body is shaking from pleasure."

He abruptly dropped his hands away from her, straightening and dragging in a breath. Not that it did him any good. Her scent still filled his nose, coated his tongue. Athena stared at him, hazel eyes hooded, her full lips parted, as if silently begging him for the corruption he'd described. And God help him, he almost gave in.

"Baby girl," he growled. "Move."

His guttural order seemed to shake her loose, because her eyes widened the tiniest bit. With a small, jerky nod, she scrambled off his thighs, launching across the room in several long strides. She halted at the window, wrapping her arms around herself, and the protective gesture wasn't lost on him. But just who did she seek to guard herself from? Him…or her?

Maybe both.

If she were prudent, both.

He rose to his feet, studying her. The same urgency, the same need that had propelled him across the couch to hold her, insisted he cross the room and take her in his arms again. But this time, he resisted that urge. Because he was the burden.

"Are you okay?" he asked.

She nodded. "I'm fine." She lowered her arms to her sides, palms up. "I'm sorry," she murmured. "I crossed a line tonight. It won't happen again."

He dipped his chin in acknowledgment. "There's nothing to apologize for. We'll chalk tonight up to emotion and let it go." Ignoring the almost tangible pull toward her, he strode in the opposite direction, grabbing his discarded tuxedo jacket from the back of a dining room chair. "I'll text you with next week's schedule."

"Okay." A pause. "Nico."

He turned to face her, his hand on the doorknob. She remained standing by the window, sorrow and weariness on her face.

"Yes?"

"Thank you. For everything. I'll never forget that."

He nodded, then opened her front door and…paused. Dammit, he needed to get out of this apartment. Get away from her before he ended up with more than the taste of her tears on his tongue. Yet, he stood there, unable to move, words he should've said months ago a weight on his heart for the woman who'd shown him kindness and trust when no one else but his mother had.

"I'm sorry about your grandmother. She was a good woman. One of the finest people I've met, and when someone like that dies, they leave a hole in this world. One that can't be filled. Maybe shouldn't be filled. She was that special. I'm glad you had her in your life, Athena. And I know she's thankful she had you."

Not glancing back over his shoulder or giving her a chance to respond, he exited, pulling the door closed behind him with a soft *snick*. For a long moment, he stood on the other side, his hand still curled around the doorknob. He closed his eyes, his grip tightening.

I'll never forget that.

Her statement shivered through him like a warning, a threat.

Because he needed her to forget, to not treat him any differently than the uneasy, wary partners they'd become. Partners who didn't trust each other and would separate, returning to their own lives at the end of this.

Anything different, and he would start to forget himself.

And that, he couldn't allow.

Eight

The desk phone intercom buzzed, interrupting Nico's concentration. Dragging his gaze from the Farrell International report on the Bromberg's renovation. So far, the project was surpassing expectations, especially with the opening of the Intimate Curves flagship store. The spark of happiness in his chest for Kenan and Eve had taken him by surprise. Nico had been there when Kenan proposed the project and praised Eve's company, holding her up as the jewel of the rebranded Bromberg's. Kenan hadn't been wrong; the investment had been sound.

That still didn't explain the "spark." Or why it suspiciously felt like pride as well as happiness.

Frowning, Nico rubbed his knuckles over the offending spot as he pressed the button on his desk phone with the other hand.

"Yes, Paul?"

"Sorry to disturb you, Mr. Morgan, but the security desk downstairs called. There's a Mr. Randall Evans here to see you, even though he doesn't have an appointment." There was no mistaking the disapproval in his executive assistant's tone. "Should I have this Mr. Evans schedule an appointment?"

Nico fell back in his office chair, staring at his closed office door. Anger simmered in his chest. His fingers curled into his palms, his blunt nails biting into his flesh.

What the fuck was Randall doing here? There was absolutely no love lost between them. Of all Athena's family members, Nico had the least use for her brother.

Especially since the last time he'd seen Randall, he'd threatened to ruin Nico's planned proposal unless Nico handed over money for his latest get-rich-quick scheme.

Threatened, hell. It'd been a promise. One he'd followed through on.

Athena was responsible for her own choices, and she'd chosen to blow them up. But her brother had lit the match.

So what the hell was he doing here? According to Athena, she hadn't told Randall about their arrangement.

Firming his mouth, he punched the intercom button again. Only one way to find out.

"Tell security to bring him upstairs."

"Yes, sir."

Nico rose from his chair, fastening the button on his suit jacket, the flame of impending battle alight in his veins. Maybe he didn't know Randall's purpose, but he harbored zero doubts it had something to do with money or an asinine scheme. Three years had passed since they'd last had contact, but the man hadn't changed that much. As proven by his taking a loan out behind his family's back.

No, Randall Evans hadn't changed at all.

Within minutes, a knock sounded on Nico's office door and he rounded his desk just as Paul opened the door and stepped inside, Randall behind him.

"Mr. Morgan, Mr. Evans is here to see you," his assistant said, stepping to the side and allowing Randall entrance. "Do you need coffee, tea or water?"

Randall smiled and parted his lips to answer, but Nico shook his head.

"No, thank you. Mr. Evans won't be here that long."

The other man's expression darkened, whether from embarrassment or anger, Nico didn't know. And frankly, didn't give a damn.

"Thank you, Paul."

His executive assistant nodded and exited the office.

"What do you want, Randall?" Fuck the pleasantries.

Nico wouldn't call Randall's baring of teeth a smile. Maybe if fury didn't glitter in his dark eyes, he could've achieved it.

"It's nice to see you again, too, Nico." Randall's laugh held a tight quality that belied his claim. "I was surprised to find out you and my sister were back together. We're a very close family, as you know, so imagine my shock when my mother mentioned it." Randall cocked his head and rocked back on his heels. "I can't lie, though. I have my concerns about the renewal of this relationship. And I expressed those concerns to Athena. But as her brother, I'm supportive…to a point."

"How about you get to that point?" Nico asked, injecting a note of boredom in his voice even as his anger crackled. To anyone else, Randall Evans might pass as the "supportive" brother he called himself. But Nico knew him for the grasping, greedy and self-entitled asshole he truly was. "You dropped by my office without an appointment. And I only agreed to see you out of curiosity, not loyalty to your sister. Because let's be honest, since it's just us—you have no loyalty to her. Or anyone else, for that matter. So how about you get to the reason you're here. I have work to do."

Once more, irritation ghosted over the other man's features before he seemed to catch himself. Apparently, Randall believed he would stroll into this office and control the conversation. The man possessed a nearly sociopathic narcissism to believe people didn't see past his bullshit. Just two nights ago, he'd left his sister emotionally bruised because of his emotional manipulations.

The sad part?

His family would let him continue on, business as usual.

Even after his bargain with Athena ended and Nico paid off Randall's loan, Athena would continue to run the bakery in his stead, and his mother would keep enabling him. And Randall would face no consequences, wouldn't even be uncomfortable because of his careless decisions. Who would bail them out the next time Randall placed the business in danger? Because as sure as Barron Farrell had been a bastard, there would be a next time.

"Fine. I came here for two reasons. To ensure my sister was in good hands—" Nico snorted, and Randall's hands fisted in his pockets "—and to bring a business venture to you," he finished through clenched teeth.

"There it is," Nico murmured, crossing his arms.

His first inclination was to deliver an automatic no, and kick Randall out of his office. But again, that damn curiosity. Not that he had any intention of investing in whatever scheme Randall proposed or handing money over to him. But this ought to be good.

"You're a smart businessman and can appreciate a good deal when you hear it," Randall said, his smile returning as he dropped compliments. As if they would make any difference with Nico. "I have the opportunity to get into a new chain of barbershops on the ground floor. These are going to be special. Each shop staffed with only the top barbers, stylists and manicurists. They will offer not just cuts but grooming services and hair-care products. These will be the premier places to go for self-care and pampering."

The enthusiasm coloring his voice glittered in his eyes. And if it'd been anyone else but Randall, Nico's interest might've been piqued. But it *was* Randall. And Nico didn't trust the other man.

"And?" Nico pressed, certain there was more to it.

"And I need one hundred thousand to invest in the project. When the shops are up and running, you'll receive your money back. This is a can't-fail investment!"

"Oh really?" Nico arched an eyebrow. "Anytime someone says the words *can't-fail investment* I get suspicious because no such thing exists. What makes your barbershops different from other full-service establishments? What demographic are you targeting? Where is the business plan?" Nico extended his hand, palm up. "You can't just come in here asking me for one hundred thousand dollars on the basis of your smile and sister's connection."

Randall's face darkened. "It's a sound business project. I've examined it from every angle and we already have several investors. This is personal."

Nico snorted again. "You're damn right it is. You didn't come here in a professional capacity. If you did, you would've scheduled an appointment and had a proposal with projections for me to analyze. This whole thing—" he flicked a hand back and forth between them "—is personal. In addition, you're not asking me to be an investor. You're the investor and you're expecting me to front you the money."

"So you want me to sign something? Fine." He gestured in the direction of Nico's desk. "Draw up something and I'll sign it, promising to pay you back."

The corner of Nico's mouth curled. "Somehow I doubt a piece of paper would hold you to your word about repayment if this fell through."

Case in point, the copy of the banknote with Randall's signature in his desk drawer.

"You weren't even trying to hear my idea, were you?" Randall sneered. "What's one hundred thousand dollars to you? A drop in the bucket? Still the same selfish bastard you were three years ago."

Nico dipped his chin in acknowledgment. "Game recognizes game," he praised. "Now that my curiosity's been satisfied, you can go. I have a meeting in ten minutes."

He turned to head back to his desk but Randall's sly voice stopped him.

"You're so cocky, think your shit can't be touched. But remember what happened last time. I called all the shots. You had plans that involved my sister. A proposal, if my memory serves me right. And how did that turn out when you didn't give me what I asked for? I wrecked that shit. So you can look down on me all you want, but I hold all the power here. I can fuck you up again if you don't hand over what I want. And we both know who Athena really listens to. If you don't want a repeat of last time, I need a check for a hundred thousand by the end of the week."

Nico slowly pivoted, facing Randall again, studying his smug smile and gleaming dark brown eyes as if from the distance of a long tunnel.

In that tunnel, images from that evening came at him in Technicolor with full sound, drilling into his head and eyes, blinding and deafening him.

Randall, arriving at his penthouse and asking for a loan for another get-rich-quick business venture much like today, and Nico denying him.

Randall, spotting the small, dark blue velvet box with the ring Nico had bought for Athena.

Randall, threatening him, that if Nico didn't give him the money, he would get Athena to leave Nico.

Athena, walking out a week later.

A heat born of hurt, resentment and grief swirled through him, ripping through the memories like flames through paper. Leaving blackened edges and ash behind.

Only one thing prevented the fire from blazing out of control, from consuming both him and Randall.

Randall couldn't influence Athena into abandoning him this time. Not when the bakery and Randall's ass were on the line. She wouldn't leave Nico before the three months were up. Not before he accomplished his goal.

Then he would let her go. He would be the one to walk.

Caustic laughter scratched at his throat. Oh the irony. Randall's thirst for money and power prevented Athena from leaving Nico now, when three years ago, it'd been his weapon to influence her to go.

"You're so confident of your sway over your sister, Randall," Nico murmured. "A little overconfident, I think." He tipped his chin up, allowing a hard, cruel smile to curl his mouth. "Give it your best shot. Because you're not getting one dime from me. Now—" he made a show of flipping his wrist over and glancing at his watch "—I really do have to end this meeting, as…entertaining as it's been. You know the way out."

Turning again, Nico didn't bother looking back as he strode across the room to his desk. Only once he was seated did he spare the other man a glance, and that was to see him disappear through the office door.

Nico propped his elbows on the arms of his chair and templed his fingers underneath his chin. He wasn't fool enough to believe this was the last he'd see or hear from Randall Evans.

Not by a long shot.

Nine

"Whoa," Athena breathed.

Oh how she wished something a little more sophisticated had passed through her lips, but she couldn't manage more. The historic Beacon Hill mansion of white stone had large bay windows, sconces and honest-to-God turrets.

"It's something, isn't it?" Nico drawled from beside her, his hand cupping her elbow.

She tore her gaze away from the monument to excess and glanced up at Nico. His face rivaled the stone before them.

"*Something* is a good word for it." She tilted her head. "Is this your first time visiting your father's home?"

Nico blinked, dragging his hooded stare from the mansion and dropping it to her.

"Yes."

His abrupt answer didn't invite discussion, but she'd warned him she'd do everything in her power to convince him this path of revenge was destructive.

So, she pushed.

"Are you okay with going in there?" she asked. "Up until now, you've been little more than a business acquaintance. Kenan and Eve would understand if you left an apology about not being able to make it."

"Why should I have a problem entering into Barron's, now Cain's, house?" His mouth curved. "Because my father has never allowed me to enter its hallowed halls before? Tell me, Athena," he murmured, lowering his head, the scent of whiskey and the red licorice he used to eat ghosting over her lips. "Are you concerned my feelings will be hurt?"

"You'd have to possess feelings first," she muttered. He snorted, and she shook her elbow free, looping her arm under his and gently clasping his hand. "Doesn't matter if you want to admit it or not. I'm here with you tonight. We'll get through this together."

This being facing the past, the childhood years that he and his mother could've enjoyed had Barron been a man of integrity, or just owned a soul. Undoubtedly, Nico didn't want her support—or believed he didn't need it—but he had no choice. He'd provided for her grandmother until the day she left this earth; Athena would pay that debt. But not by assisting him in stealing his father's, now his brothers', company.

No, Glory Evans cherished family, and if she could repay Nico for his generosity, it would be with that gift. So Athena would do it in her grandmother's stead. Nico believed he needed revenge to be whole; she'd return to him what Barron had truly stolen from him—his brothers.

"So we're a team, now?" he asked, his cynicism so thick it was a wonder he didn't choke on it.

"I realize that suspicion must serve you well in business, but it must be hell on real-life relationships."

Case in point, theirs. If only he'd opened his heart to her, they might've had a shot at something real, something lasting. But water under the bridge now. *Everything doesn't only happen for a reason, but for a purpose and a plan*, Mama used to say. And as painful as the ending of Athena's relationship with Nico had been, she'd saved herself from the devastating pain of falling deeper in love with him, if she'd stayed longer.

Nico Morgan wasn't a man to be trusted with a woman's heart—not if she didn't want it returned in jagged pieces.

"You're lucky I have a naturally optimistic personality," she continued. "Because you could drive a saint to a drunk and disorderly charge."

"Well good thing you're not a saint, isn't it?"

Heat sizzled up her bare arms and down her spine, which was completely exposed by her red lace, sleeveless, floor-length gown. She tried to drag her gaze away from his, but that dark, knowing stare might as well as have been a hard grip. She *couldn't* avoid it. Neither could she avoid the images bombarding her. Just days ago, she'd perched on his lap, holding his hand to her mouth. Kissing that hand. Tasting that sandalwood and earthy musk that belonged only to him.

Pushing him.

So it'd been for the best that he'd pumped the brakes.

Best for both of them. The last thing either of them needed was this bargain muddied by sex.

But that clear, cold logic didn't halt the march of lust. If a shattered heart and three years' absence didn't do the impossible, hell, most likely nothing would. She just had to accept that. Didn't mean she had to act on this clawing, relentless hunger, though.

No matter how bad it ached—

The peal of her phone pierced the night air, and she flinched at the jarring sound even as she breathed a sigh of relief. Fingers fumbling, she popped open her clutch and removed her cell. One glance at the screen squelched the relief, replacing it with annoyance and dread.

What. Now?

Grimacing, she glanced up at Nico. "I'm sorry, I need to take this. It'll be quick." If possible, Nico's obsidian eyes darkened even more, but he gave her a terse nod. Ducking her head, she swept her thumb over the screen and lifted the phone to her ear—convincing herself that the twisting in her stomach was not due to her feeling as if she'd disappointed him. "Yes, Randall?"

"Good evening to you, too, sis."

Closing her eyes, she pinched the bridge of her nose. They hadn't spoken since that morning at the bakery, so what could he want with her? Especially at eight o'clock at night.

"I'm in the middle of something, Randall, so if you could just tell me what you need?"

His abrupt chuckle echoed in her ear. "Let me guess. Out on the date with your millionaire?" She didn't need to see her brother's face to hear the sneer in his voice. "So that means no time for your family?"

God, not this. Again.

"I'm answering my phone, right? What do you need?" she asked, not masking her impatience. Damn, how could an almost thirty-year-old man still behave like a spoiled toddler?

And frankly, she was being a little unfair to the toddler.

"Since you asked so nicely," he mocked. "Listen, Mom is going through Mama's things tonight, and we need you to come home and be with her."

Hurt and grief seized her chest, squeezing and squeezing until she had to, by force of will, smother her pained gasp. She lifted a fist to her chest, as if she could massage her breaking heart. In the months since her grandmother had passed, none of them had been strong enough to go through her clothes, knickknacks, jewelry and other belongings.

For Mom to do it now… What happened? What changed? Was she okay—

A large hand cupped the nape of her neck, and the warm, solid weight of it grounded her. Yes, she might regret it later, but here, in this moment, she leaned back into that strength, depended on it. Borrowing just a little of it.

Opening her eyes, she stared ahead at the Beacon Hill mansion, but in her head, she saw the cheery, cozy room where her grandmother would sit by the window, playing solitaire the old-fashioned way—with actual cards—or organizing her coin collection.

God, Athena missed her. And she needed her, more than ever.

"Athena? Did you hear me? We need you to come home."

Drawing in a trembling breath, she shook her head, even though Randall couldn't see it. "I can't right now. I'll go by to see her tomorrow, though. Make sure she's okay."

"What?" Randall barked, his fury nearly pulsating down the connection. "I said Mom needs you. Fuck who you're out with. This is our mother. Get here. Now."

Anger poured through her like gasoline, his words and tone a match tossed on it. Who the hell did he think he was talking to?

"Excuse me?" she said, her grip on her phone tightening until the edges bit into her fingers. "I think you forgot it's me, your sister, you're talking to, not your wife, not your daughter. As I said, I cannot cancel my plans tonight, especially on such short notice. And as hard as going through Mama's belongings are, Mom isn't alone. She has you, Kira and Dad there with her."

"It's not the same," he snapped. "And besides, I'm not home at the moment—"

"Oh really?" She stiffened, that fury snapping hard inside her. "Well, let me give you the same advice you offered me. Get home *now*. Your family needs you. Good night, Randall."

Ending the call, she turned the ringer off. It immediately lit up again with a call from her brother, but she dropped the cell in her purse and snapped it shut.

"Sorry about that," she said, forcing her lips to curve into a smile. "It won't hap—"

"Are you okay?" Nico's hold on her didn't shift, didn't ease up.

"I'm—" The *fine* stalled on her tongue, halted by the sharp gaze studying her features. "Pissed. So damn pissed. And hurting for my mother at the thought of her going through my grandmother's things by herself. But I'll be okay. I'm committed to being here and not bailing, if that's your worry."

"I'm not worried about that." He flicked the hand not cradling her neck. "I am concerned about you. Your brother can be..." His eyebrows jacked down into a vee, his full lips flattening as if trapping that description of Randall behind them.

She snickered, surprised at the burst of humor.

"Look at you, trying to be diplomatic." She smirked, then sighed. "Yes, Randall can be an insufferable asshole and he was at his best just now. But I can't..." Her lips twisted. "I can't keep standing in the gap and making it okay for him to dodge his responsibility. He wants me to come home and help Mom go through our grandmother's belongings, but not once did it occur to him that he should be there. Not once did it occur to him that maybe I'm not able to do it. But Randall never considers the cost to others, just to himself."

She heaved a sigh, tipping her head back and staring up at the cloudy yet star-studded sky. Nico shifted his hand, sliding it from her neck to the small of her back. Immediately, she missed the possessiveness of his hold. But she didn't have time to dwell on the curious pull in her chest, because his palm connected with the skin bared by her backless dress. Sizzling electricity emanated from that point of contact and spasmed straight to her core. Her thighs shivered, and only pride kept her from cupping her suddenly full, sensitive breasts.

"We should probably head in," she murmured, desperate to be in front of people. An audience would prevent her betraying her resolve. Hopefully. "It's probably bad manners to show up fashionably late to an engagement party."

He dipped his chin in acknowledgment, and led her toward the mansion's gated entrance and front steps. The building impressed her even more up close. Impressed her in the way the Louvre or the Met did. As something to appreciate for its beauty and architectural features, but not as a place to live, to make a home. It lacked…warmth.

"Four generations of Farrells have lived here," Nico said, the flame from a sconce next to the door casting shadows over his profile. "I lied before. I've never been inside, but I've been here. I used to drive by as a teenager, trying to catch a glimpse of my father and his family. I don't know what I expected to happen when I finally did," he murmured, his gaze steady on the door as if even now, he was seeing the father who'd abandoned him emerge, along with the wife and the son he'd kept. "A sense of vindication? Of satisfaction? Of joy, maybe, because I'd seen him? I felt like shit. Worse than shit. That was the last time I came here."

"Until tonight." She stepped forward so his hand slipped from the base of her spine, and she reached behind her, once more tangling her fingers with his.

His scrutiny shifted down to their clasped hands, then lifted, meeting her eyes.

"Until tonight." He squeezed her fingers and didn't let go.

The front door opened, and an older man, short, with an almost regal bearing, a military straight posture and a forthright gaze, stood in the entryway.

"Good evening," he greeted with a nod of his white-haired head. "Name, please."

"Nico Morgan and Athena Evans," Nico supplied.

The man must've had a guest list in his head, because he stepped back and permitted them entrance.

"Welcome to Mr. Rhodes and Ms. Burke's engagement party." The older man closed the door and moved farther into the huge foyer.

Athena's heels clicked over a pristine marble floor. Above them, light from a crystal chandelier rivaled the sun. Artwork in ornate frames hung from the walls and, contrary to the cold, intimidating appearance of the building outside, the area was inviting. Lovely, comfortable-looking armchairs and chaise lounges dotted the area, welcoming guests to sit a moment while surrendering their coats or mingling.

"If you'll follow me, I'll show you to the other guests," the man said, turning and heading down the hall that passed a stunning marble staircase.

"Thank you," Nico said.

They followed, clasped hands between them, her knuckles brushing his powerful thigh. A small caress, but it pulsed through her. Tempted her to straighten her fingers, turn her hand around and feel that strong, flexing muscle against her skin.

She might have a thing for his long, toned legs.

In moments, the older gentleman paused at the entrance to a large room that could've been a ballroom. About sixty tuxedoed and gowned guests were gathered, their chatter and laughter filling the air. A spirit of gaiety filled the space, and it didn't strike her as forced or fake. The people here, smiling and drinking champagne, seemed to actually delight in being here, celebrating Kenan and Eve and their impending marriage.

From her time in Nico's world, this...genuine happiness for someone else was rare.

And inspiring.

She scanned the crowd for the engaged couple, and soon located them at the other end of the room. A smile that started deep in her chest spread across her face. Though they were surrounded by well-wishers, Kenan's arm circled Eve's shoulders, cradling her into his side. And she leaned into him, her trust and love evident. If the room had plunged into darkness, they would beam bright like a beacon.

The thrust of envy between the ribs caught Athena by surprise. There'd been a time when she'd worn love like that. When she'd been sure anyone glancing at her would see adoration in her eyes, on her very skin, like sun reflecting off glass.

Oh God, if she'd stayed longer, Nico could've owned her heart and soul.

She'd wanted him to.

She would've gladly given him all of her if he would've just given all of himself in return.

That was a lie.

If Nico would've offered even a sliver of himself, she wouldn't have left. Maybe they would be celebrating their engagement now. Or even a marriage.

The hell, Athena. Get it together.

Giving her head a hard mental shake, she jerked her enraptured gaze from Kenan and Eve. She couldn't afford to drop her guard and slide down the slippery slope of the past.

She didn't trust herself.

"Look at you!" The excited feminine voice tore her from her morose thoughts. Athena almost moaned in relief when Devon approached her, arms outstretched, beautiful in an emerald green, empire waist, halter top gown. Devon cupped Athena's arms and beamed up at her. "You're gorgeous. This dress is amazing."

Athena fought not to glide her palms down the red silk and lace gown that fit like it had been stitched onto her. With a deep neckline in the front and a nonexistent back, the dress was more revealing than anything she'd worn before. But the flare of lust in Nico's eyes when he'd first seen her had eased all her concerns about showing too much skin.

"Thanks," Athena said, smiling. "You, too. I love your dress, and you look hot."

Devon grinned. "Aw, go on you flatterer, you. Cain certainly thought so." She wiggled her eyebrows, and Athena snickered.

"I'm going to get a drink. Athena, would you like one?" Nico interrupted.

Athena shot him a glance. "Sounding a little desperate there, buddy."

His expression remained stoic but she didn't miss the faint quirk of his lips. "Not at all. I just can't have my fiancée dying of thirst."

She released a bark of laughter, not caring if it was

considered gauche. "Right. But I'll grant you a reprieve. I'd like a glass of Moscato, please."

He nodded. "Mrs. Farrell?"

"Oh please, Devon." She shook her head, holding up a nearly full glass and grinned at him. "Sparkling cider. Thank you, though. And I apologize for traumatizing you."

"No worries. Whiskey will help me forget," he said, tone smooth.

Devon cackled. "Good thing we serve only the good stuff."

"I'll be right back."

He turned and disappeared into the crowd, and Athena stared after his tall, powerful figure. A tender pang resonated in her chest, and she tightened her grip on her purse—either that or rub the spot and admit that it might be there because she missed him by her side. Missed the intimate pressure of his hand wrapped around hers. She curled her fingers into her palm.

Was this the beginning of her downfall? Of her plunge into another heartbreak that would do just that—break her?

Fear streaked through her, jagged and lightning bright.

"Oh, hon." A small, delicate hand patted hers. Devon tsked. "I recognize that look. You're not going to be able to wait until he gets back with your wine. And you need something stronger. Let's go find it. Then you can tell me what has you terrified. Although I can guess. I fell in love with Cain Farrell, after all." The other woman looped her arm through Athena's and gently tugged her in the opposite direction of where Nico had headed.

"We've just started to get to know one another these last few weeks, but you're not alone in this."

That's where Devon was wrong.

Athena was alone.

When it came to Nico Morgan, she always had been. Always would be.

"Thanks, Mark." Nico shook hands with the distinguished older gentleman. "I'll have my executive assistant call your office next week to schedule an appointment to nail down the details."

"Sounds good." Mark Hanson clapped Nico on the shoulder, smiling broadly. "I look forward to hearing from you. Good doing business with you, Nico."

"Same here."

With a nod, Nico continued on the path toward the bar that had been interrupted by the businessman. Not that the disruption hadn't been welcome. He'd been trying to close a deal with Mark Hanson for over a month. And now it seemed the deal was steps from being closed. The other man had been eyeing a telecommunications company Nico's corporation owned. Nico had only been willing to part with it at the right price, and those seven figures included five of Mark's Farrell International shares. It'd required some negotiating, but just now, they'd come to an agreement.

Which meant, only six more shares stood between him and control of his father's company.

Fierce satisfaction should fill him. Or at the very least, anticipation. But as he wound through the crowds of people, nodding at those he knew, only a grim, hollow resolve yawned wide in his gut. This was what he

had to do, the road to justice, but the pleasure he'd expected… He gave his head a small, hard shake.

Where the fuck was it?

He deserved it.

Unbidden, he glanced across the room toward Kenan
and Eve. At the very obvious love that damn near emanated from them. Nico's private investigator had been
very thorough, so he knew their complete story. And
they deserved *that*. For however long it lasted. Because
in his experience, it wouldn't survive the test of time
and hardship. But for their sake, he almost hoped it
would…

"They're disgustingly happy, right?"

Nico jerked his attention from the engaged couple
to meet Cain's blue-gray eyes. As in every occasion
when he'd come in contact with his half brothers, Nico's
heart thundered against his rib cage. Cain, especially.
Because he had been the boy Nico had once watched
from afar. The one he'd envied for so long. The chosen
one, while Nico had been the castoff.

Part of him wanted to study Cain, discover what
made him so lovable and worthy that Barron kept him
and raised him. So Nico could do…what? Emulate those
qualities? It was too late, but still… That insatiably curious boy in him refused to let it go. And that same little,
lonely boy who'd desired a brother couldn't stop being
nervous around this man. So Nico hid those feelings behind reserve. While he'd warmed up a little with Kenan
and even Achilles, who made Nico look like a Chatty
Cathy, Cain dragged him back to that vulnerable, *hurt*
boy, and it scared him.

And now here Nico stood, unable to avoid Cain or that piercing Farrell stare.

Desperate for that whiskey, Nico stepped up to the full-service bar.

"Whiskey. Neat. A glass of Moscato." Then, arching a brow at Cain, he drawled, "This said from the man whose wife drove me to drinking with comments of just how hot you find her."

Cain smirked. "She's not wrong."

"Jesus," Nico muttered, reaching for his tumbler filled with the amber alcohol. "I should've ordered a double."

Laughing, Cain clapped him on the shoulder. "Sorry."

"Somehow, I don't get 'sorry' off you," Nico said, eyes narrowed.

Cain shrugged, an unrepentant smile curving his mouth. "I tried." He paused as Nico took Athena's glass of wine. "Thank you for coming to the party. We've been business associates for a while, but Eve has really come to like Athena. So has Devon and Mycah. I'm sure it means a lot to her that you two are here for their engagement party."

"You're welcome. It's our pleasure."

Cain fell silent and his bright scrutiny moved over Nico. By sheer will, he didn't frown or demand to know what the fuck he was looking at? Yeah, he might be a little defensive. Finally, Cain shook his head, a rueful smile touching his lips.

"I'm sorry, that was rude, and I promised Devon I'd work on that. It's just that you look familiar to me. You always have, and I just can't put my finger on it…"

Panic and, dammit, just a little excitement, clawed at him. Who did Cain glimpse when he looked at Nico? Himself? Their father? What if he figured out their connection? No, Nico didn't want that. Not yet.

Right?

Damn, *no*. No, *he didn't*.

"Thank you, Cain. Thank you very much," Achilles growled, approaching them, his giant frame parting people like a biblical miracle.

With amusement that he hid behind a sip of whiskey, Nico watched as guests regarded the large, scowling man with wariness, despite his flawlessly tailored suit.

"What did I do?" Cain lifted his hands. "I've just been standing here. Nico is my witness. Tell him." He dipped his head toward Achilles.

Nico shrugged, taking another sip from his tumbler. "Depends. What're you offering for my cooperation?"

"Wow. Really?" Cain scowled, but the gleam of amusement in his eyes belied the frown.

"No, you're guilty because your wife is guilty." Achilles jabbed a finger at Cain. "You know how much I hate these things and Mycah is my lifeline. And Devon comes along and shanghais her for some 'girl time,' whatever the fuck that means. Her, my wife and your fiancée—" he jerked his chin up at Nico "—have disappeared, probably to talk all kinds of shit about us. Which means all three of us will no doubt be paying for old and new tonight. This is a fucking engagement party, Cain. *Engage* your wife."

Nico blinked, caught between laughter and shock. That was the most he'd heard Achilles speak in one breath since he'd met his younger half brother.

Cain lifted a hand again, palm up. "I'd go find her but I'm on parent watch."

Achilles's expression cleared, his broad shoulders drawing back with tension. "Right. How's that going?" He shifted to the other side of Nico and plucked the wineglass from his hand. "I'm guessing this is for Athena? She won't be needing it." Achilles sipped it, grimaced, then took another sip. "Nothing beats a good Guinness."

"So far, so good," Cain answered Achilles's question. He shot a glance at Nico. "Sorry, I'm being rude again. Kenan's parents are here tonight."

"They're not happy about the marriage?" Surprise winged through Nico. Not only at this news—Eve was wonderful—but that Cain and Achilles so openly shared it with him.

"It's complicated," Achilles muttered. "But the mom's okay. It's his father who's just not…happy. So we're on interference duty. Like—*fuck*. Now."

"Well damn," Cain muttered, striding across the room.

Achilles charged after him, and for some inexplicable reason, Nico followed.

In moments, they reached Kenan and Eve just as an older couple and a handsome younger Black man did. Kenan still wore the smile he'd been wearing all evening, but it seemed strained and his blue-gray eyes had dimmed, losing that gleam of happiness. Eve turned to the couple Nico assumed were Kenan's parents and smiled, sliding her arm around Kenan's waist.

"Hi, Nathan and Dana. I'm so glad you could make it tonight. The occasion wouldn't have been complete without all of our family here to celebrate with us." She turned to the younger man with them and her smile warmed. "And of course, you, too, Gavin. Thank you for being here."

"Of course," Gavin said. "Do I get to kiss my soon-to-be sister-in-law?" He glanced at Kenan, grinning. "What do you say, Kenan? Or am I risking a broken face?"

Kenan squinted. "Possibly. But I'm feeling magnanimous."

"Uh, hello." Eve waved. "Agency here." She laughed. Stepping forward, she hugged the other man and kissed him on the cheek. "It's good to see you."

"Mom," Kenan said and held his arms open.

Nico caught the flash of relief that flickered across the lovely older woman's face before she moved into her son's embrace. They hugged, and Nico almost turned away from the emotion that crossed Kenan's mother's face. Regret, sorrow and a deep love.

In that moment, his own arms ached with emptiness. Times like this, he missed his mother with a strength that threatened to drag him to his knees. He'd never get to hold her again, inhale her scent or hear her voice. And it struck him like a punch to the gut. He stiffened his spine and breathed deep, deliberate.

A shoulder nudged his and stayed there, not moving. As if propping him up. Nico glanced to his left and Achilles stood next to him, not looking at him but was…there.

Right.

If anyone would understand the loss of a mother, it would be him.

He should move; he didn't need this support. Especially from a stranger. Their father's DNA might connect them, but Achilles didn't know that.

But Nico didn't move away.

And in this moment, he chose not to analyze why.

"Hey, Dad." Kenan turned to his father and extended a hand. "Thanks for coming."

His father accepted it, then quickly let go. "Thank you for inviting us. I was pleasantly surprised to be included, since I wasn't sure we were still considered a part of your family." He flicked pointed looks at Cain and Achilles, his lips curling in disdain.

Well…damn.

That'd been rude as hell.

"Nathan," Kenan's mother murmured, pink tingeing her high cheekbones.

"Come on, Dad," Gavin admonished with a frown. "Not tonight."

But Nathan's expression hardened, and his family's appeals had the effect of pebbles bouncing off a brick wall. One glance at the anger and pain flashing in Kenan's eyes and Eve clutching his arm, and Nico jumped in.

"If I'm not mistaken, you're Nathan and Dana Rhodes of Rhodes Realty?" Nico stepped forward, his hand outstretched toward Kenan's mother first, who shook it, and then his father, who, still frowning, repeated the gesture. "I apologize for the interruption, but I'm Nico Morgan. I own Brightstar Holdings, LLC. Perhaps you've heard of it?"

Nathan's frown disappeared and he nodded, his entire demeanor changing from combative to amiable.

"Of course. It's a pleasure to meet you, Mr. Morgan."

"Nico, please. I've admired your company's work and reputation for a long time now. I realize it's your son's engagement party, but I also believe in serendipity— or taking advantage of an opportunity." Nico smiled. "Would you mind if I stole you away? Kenan? Are you okay if I borrow your dad? Just for a few moments."

"Uh, no," Kenan said with a shake of his head. The corner of his mouth lifted and he slid an arm around Eve's shoulders. "I don't mind. You fine with that, Eve?"

"Our family using any occasion for business? Shocker." She beamed, and if Nico wasn't mistaken, gratitude shone from her eyes. "No, it's okay. You two go. But don't forget us."

Nico nodded and stepped toward Nathan, sweeping an arm. "Nathan, how about a drink? I hear they're free," he said, earning the chuckle he'd been after.

As he and Kenan's father walked away from the group and Nico launched into a business pitch, his pulse hammered. Eve hadn't meant him when she'd mentioned "family." But in that instant, it'd felt like it. And the glide of warmth that had slid through his veins unsettled him.

Because in that same instant, he'd craved being a member of that family.

Ten

Athena stared ahead at the privacy divide separating the front of the limousine from the rear, where she and Nico sat.

A very quiet Nico.

She peeked at him from the corner of her eye. He'd been lost inside himself since she'd emerged from the study with Devon and Mycah, where she'd enjoyed a brandy and the other two had sipped on glasses of sparkling cider. The impromptu girls' session where they'd regaled her with stories about their relationships and gently probed her about her own "romance" had been fun. And though Athena had kept up the charade and suffered guilt at her lying, she'd rejoined the party more in love than ever with Devon and Mycah.

But her delight had been dimmed by Nico's reserve. It wasn't obvious. No, to everyone else, he appeared as charming and polite as always. But she noticed the difference. Noted the stiffness. As if one touch would shatter him like glass.

What the hell happened?

The question burned on her tongue like a live coal. But the last time she broached a subject about his family, he'd shut her down. And it'd hurt.

Risking another peek, she studied him. The taut pull of skin over his chiseled cheekbones. The hooded, forward-focused stare. The rigid set of his frame. The almost too relaxed spread of his fingers along his thighs.

Pain. It reverberated through him. Self-preservation screamed leave it and him alone. But her foolish, suicidal heart...

Hell.

"Nico?"

"Yes?"

She waited several seconds.

"Look at me, please."

His chin jerked and he turned his head, his onyx gaze fixing on her.

"You wanted my attention, baby girl. Now you have it."

"Don't do that," she murmured. "Don't shut me out."

"Is that what I'm doing?"

"You know you are." She shook her head. "But it won't work. Not this time." Risking rejection, she laid her hand on his leg. "Talk to me."

His jaw worked as if it struggling with the words. He lowered his gaze to her hand, studying it. And when he finally met her eyes again, the impact nearly shoved her back against the seat. So much anger, sorrow, grief, fear...need.

They all blazed in those eyes.

If she possessed the sense God gave a gnat, she'd let it go.

But apparently, when it came to this man, she had zero wisdom.

"Please let me in," she whispered.

How many times had she said that same thing to herself when they'd been together? So many, it'd become her personal mantra. And each time, she'd never believed he would. And if she were honest, she didn't believe he would now either.

Letting loose a soft sigh, she slid her hand off his thigh—

His hand covered hers, holding it in place, pressing it to the thick muscle underneath.

She froze, her fingers curling into him out of reflex or...need.

Oh God, what was she doing? Again?

"You want in," he said, his voice a low rumble that stroked over her skin, leaving pebbled flesh behind. "Are you sure about that? Because it's not a place of sunshine and roses. It's ugly. It's scary. Half the time, I don't want to be there either. You still 'want in,' Athena?"

"Yes," she said, without hesitation.

His jaw worked again, his eyes glittered brighter under the passing streetlamps. But he shifted, leaned forward, still keeping her hand prisoner under his.

"I'm filled with hate," he growled. "For Barron for fucking my mother and me over. For my mother for

dying. For you for leaving. For my brothers for…for…"
His mouth snapped shut, his eyebrows arrowing down
above his nose.

"For having what you've always wanted," she whispered. "For making you feel."

"Yes," he agreed, the answer blunt, unadorned. "Tonight, seeing them together, celebrating one of their
own, having each other's backs, with their wives… It
reminded me of everything I could've had. Everything
that, at one time, I longed for. Things that were within
my grasp but slipped through my fingers." He lifted up
his other hand and stared at his spread fingers, as if seeing ghostly images sifting through them. "Them." He
looked at her again, and she swallowed a whimper at
the pain that spasmed across his face. "They were those
things. Brothers. Someone to be in the fire with you.
Someone who unconditionally supported and loved you.
Someone who saw you, the real you with all your flaws
and bullshit, and accepted you anyway. Someone who
offered a place to belong." His heavy breathing filled
the interior. "They could've been that for me. I saw that
tonight. I *felt* that tonight. It also hit me that if not for
a will and the spite of one old man, I could've had it."

"Nico," she breathed.

But he didn't hear her. So caught up in his head, in
the past, in his pain.

"What did I do, besides *be fucking born*, that made
my own father hate me so much? What did he see? What
did he know that he deemed me unworthy of even ac-
knowledging after death? Of giving me brothers, family? I want to go down to that cemetery, dig that old

bastard up and ask him, because I need to know. God-
dammit, I need—"

"Stop it." She yanked her hand out from under his
and cupped his face between her palms. "Stop. It. I
won't let you use Barron Farrell as the yardstick you
measure yourself by. Just hearing you call him a father
turns my stomach, so I refuse to allow you to go down
this road where his warped opinion matters."

Nico gently cuffed her wrists and tugged her hands
away from his face. A face that had hardened into an
aloof mask but whose eyes, swirling with shadows, belied that coldness.

"Thank you, Athena," he murmured. "I appr—"

"No." In moments, she wiggled and hiked her skirt to
around her thighs and straddled his lap. His big hands
gripping her hips—to move her, to hold her, she didn't
know—and she squeezed her legs around him. "No,"
she repeated.

"Dammit, Athena," he rumbled. "What the hell are
you doing?"

"Not letting you dismiss me."

She lowered her face to his, the heat from his anger
licking her skin. But that didn't stop her from trailing
her fingertips over the sharp arch of his cheekbone, the
arrogant slope of his nose, the lean planes of his cheeks.
She drew short of touching the bottom curve of his
mouth. But her fingers tingled in objection.

Cradling his face once more, she tipped his head
back. "Barron abandoning you and Rhoda had nothing to do with you or your mother. Some men have the
paternal instincts of a quokka. Barron is one of them.
Has it occurred to you that maybe Barron rejected you

because he was jealous? You are everything he could never be. You earned your success by your own hard work, sweat and perseverance, not because of your name and someone handing it down to you. Present bargain notwithstanding, you're honest. You have integrity and are respected. With all his money and power, Barron had none of that and couldn't buy it. And it probably ate at him to no end that he had nothing to do with you ending up to be the man you are. So instead of being proud of his son, Barron tried to destroy everything in you that he could never have. A good reputation. The company you built. Your mother's security. And in the end, a family."

She brushed her thumbs over his skin, her breath hitching at the silken feel of it. She marveled over his wild, almost cruel beauty.

He *was* beauty.

"Tried, Nico. He tried to destroy. But he didn't accomplish it. Including stealing your chance for family. Your brothers are there for you. All you have to do is reach out to them. I believe they'll accept you—love you."

"Like you?" If he'd snapped it or even added an arched eyebrow, she might have returned to her side of the back seat. But the question emerged on a ruined tone. And it damn near broke her. "You knew me, slept beside me, fucked me for a year and half. And yet you still walked away. Outside of business, they've known me for what, a few weeks? If you didn't find anything good enough to keep you with me, why would they take me in?"

"Nico." She shook her head, shattered and struck speechless.

"No answer? It's okay, Athena. I already—"

She crushed her mouth to his.

Taking advantage of his parted lips, she thrust her tongue deep, moaning. The smoky bite of whiskey and ever-present red licorice greeted her, but so did *Nico*. God, she'd never forget the unique, musky, addictive taste of *him*. It'd been so long, and she'd been so damn hungry. But not just for anyone. For him. For Nico.

His grip on her hips tightened, almost bruising, and she feared he would lift her off him. But he didn't. Bright joy ricocheted inside her as he balled up her gown, dragging it higher. The cool air kissed her bare legs, the damp skin of her inner thighs...the soaking wet flesh between. He tugged her forward, and her breasts pressed to his chest, her sex ground against the rigid length of his cock.

Pleasure, wild and raw, raced through her, setting off long-dormant nerve endings. She awakened with a brutal snap of fire, and cried out with it. She'd missed this consuming, nearly overwhelming hunger. Out of necessity, she'd buried this side of herself, but with one kiss, one glide of his beautiful cock over her core, he'd resurrected her.

Nico swallowed her cry, trading it for a low, rumbling groan. It rolled into her mouth, vibrated against her breasts, drawing her nipples into taut, aching peaks.

"Give me more," she begged, but the plea had barely left her lips before she took his mouth again.

Or tried to.

Nico cupped her chin in a careful, unyielding grip. That hold—possessive, dominant—had need twisting in her lower belly. She tried to shake her head, to clear it of the haze of lust clouding it, but she couldn't. He wouldn't allow it.

And damn if that didn't have her squirming in his lap.

"More of what? Be specific, baby girl," he ordered, onyx eyes glittering. "More of this?"

He nipped her bottom lip, then plunged into her mouth, his tongue dueling with hers in an erotic battle. When he lifted his head, she tried to chase him, but his hold prevented it. She glared at him, frustration a beast within her. He chuckled, the sound wicked, dirty.

"Or more of this?"

His hand on her hip firmed, pressed her down as he stroked up. His dick made a mockery of her thong, rendering it irrelevant as he ground against her folds and the tiny bundle of nerves cresting her sex.

"Oh God," she breathed, her head falling back on her shoulders. Heat engulfed her, fanning from between her thighs, speeding up her spine, into her breasts, her belly before sizzling down to the very soles of her feet.

Was she so primed for pleasure, for his touch, that one nudge to her clit would send her over the edge into release?

Yes. If the way her body lit up like a damn torch was any indication, then yes, she was.

"Which one, baby girl?" He grazed a kiss over her lips, her chin. Rolled his hips. "Do I fuck this mouth or do I let you get the front of my pants even wetter?"

Oh damn. That dirty mouth should be outlawed. Or knighted for heroic deeds.

"Why can't I have both?" She tunneled her fingers through his thick, black waves, tugging them away from his face, glorying in the silken glide over her fingers. This, she'd missed, too. "Give me both."

She couldn't be sure, but delight flashed in his eyes. The smile that curved his mouth was all hunger...and promise.

"Greedy," he murmured, his fingers caressing her jaw. "One of the things I enjoyed about you most."

Enjoyed. Not loved.

The prick of pain sliced true, but she firmly smothered it. Nothing in this moment had to do with love. They'd had their chance at that and lost it. Right now, as he molded his mouth to hers, licking it, sucking and owning it, while guiding her to ride him, the pursuit of satisfaction reigned.

Soon, prickles tingled at the back of her neck, danced down her spine and gathered at the base. Hips stuttering, a choked cry escaped her, but she didn't need words, didn't need to explain.

"Take it, Athena," Nico encouraged. "Take the edge off." Even as he spoke, he lowered his other hand between them and slipped underneath the band of her panties, unerringly locating the sensitive, stiff button. "But the next time is mine. You come around me." He firmly circled, giving her just the right amount of pressure.

In seconds, she exploded.

She cried out, arching into his fingers, riding the ridge of his dick. The tight, cresting pleasure was good, so good, but not enough.

Not nearly enough.

As soon as the shudders eased from her body, Nico slid his fingers into his mouth, licking her from his skin. His lashes fluttered down, and that quick hunger flashed inside her as if she hadn't just orgasmed moments earlier.

"That dress have a zipper?" he growled.

Instead of answering, she moved her hands to the hidden clasp and zipper at her side. Lowering it, she slid the straps down her arms, baring herself to him. Maybe modesty should've filled her as his gaze roamed over her breasts. Maybe she should've at least attempted to cover herself.

But it didn't, and she didn't.

She wanted Nico to see her, to want her. She exulted in witnessing those full, beautiful lips flatten in lust, and twin flags of color slash across his cheekbones. Watching his eyes become hooded. His need had haunted her dreams, and seeing it again in real life…

Oh no. She wanted to see it.

His mouth captured a nipple, his tongue and lips drawing on one while his fingers teased and tweaked the other.

She buried her face in his waves, whimpering, her body undulating and arching against the ecstasy he pulled from her. She'd say he worshipped her, but that would be profane. There was nothing reverent about how his tongue lapped and sucked, how his teeth raked and nipped. Nothing deferential about how his fingers molded, squeezed and twisted.

He possessed.

He corrupted.

And she loved every damn bit of it.

Lifting his head, Nico pinned her with his gaze. He

cupped the nape of her neck, pressed his mouth to hers, and she greedily opened for him, accepted his kiss.

"What more do you want?" he asked. "I'll make you come again and end this. Or I'll give you my cock and make both of us burn. Your choice."

"Make us burn," she whispered against his lips.

He tilted his head back, stared at her. Then, whatever he saw, whatever he'd sought in the first place, must've confirmed something for him, because he nodded and dropped his hands to his pants.

"Let me." She brushed his fingers aside but didn't start on the band of his tuxedo slacks.

Instead, she tugged at his bow tie, casting it aside. Next, the buttons of his shirt received her attention. When she slid that last button through its hole, she sighed, sliding her hands up his broad, hard chest. Let her fingertips sweep over the flat male nipples. Delight in their tightening. But she didn't linger there. Not when a throbbing and persistent emptiness beat inside her, insisting she fill it.

She opened the tab of his pants, jerked the zipper down, her fingers grazing his skin. His abdomen went concave, and a sharp hiss sounded above her. His thighs shifted beneath her, and his restless, hungry movements only ratcheted the need in her. Dipping her hands inside his black boxer briefs, she cupped him.

Their twin groans saturated the limousine's interior.

The hot, thick weight of him pulsed in her hands, and she couldn't resist squeezing him. Couldn't hold back from pumping him.

How could she have gone three years without touching him, having him, inhaling his scent? Even now his heavy musk teased her nose, made her mouth water for a taste. Already she could feel the heft of him on her tongue, sliding toward the back of her throat...

"No, baby girl." His hands clutched her arms, and only then did she realize she'd been on the verge of sinking to the floor between his thighs to fulfill the vision in her head. "Not this time. I want you too bad. Need to be here—" he cupped her wet, swollen sex "—too bad." Tangling his other hand in her hair again, he drew her head down until their breaths mingled, mated. "Are you sure?"

"Yes." Again, no hesitation. She had zero doubts. About this. About needing him inside her, taking away the ache.

Now about other things... God, yes. But this? No.

It was a long time coming.

Giving her that nod again, he reached into his jacket pocket and removed his wallet.

"No." She shook her head. Nico went still, his gaze on her face. "I'm on the pill. And I've been tested. You don't have a reason to believe me but I—"

"I believe you," he interrupted. And dropped the wallet to the seat beside them. Without removing a condom. "I've been tested, too." A beat of charged silence. "And I haven't been with anyone since you."

Wait. *What?*

"That's..." she started, disbelief spiraling through her like a shrieking whirlwind.

"Three years. Yes."

Why? How? Why?

The questions bombarded her, but his tongue curled

around them. And by the time he lifted his head, she didn't care about the answer. For now.

"Athena," he rumbled, one of his hands brushing both of hers aside to fist the base of his cock and hold himself. "Take me inside."

He didn't have to tell her twice. Reaching down, she looped her fingers in the band of her thong and—

Nico fisted the band and ripped it. Gripped the other side and shredded it, too.

Well, okay. That was one way to handle them.

Lifting her gaze to his, she straddled him again, her chest rising and falling, her breath whistling from between her lips. Slowly, she lowered her body until the head of him brushed her folds, her entrance.

And then he pushed inside her.

Then he was inside her.

The moan rolled out of her, pained and ecstatic. The pressure. The stretching. The *taking*. With one hand clasping the nape of her neck, pressing her forehead to his, and the other a vise grip at her hip, holding her steady as he pulsed his hips, claiming her. Conquering her. Until he left no inch of her untouched.

God, he touched her *everywhere*.

And it was beautiful.

It was everything.

Only once he was fully seated inside her, his cock an undeniable, pounding presence, did he pause, allowing her to become reaccustomed to him.

As if she could ever become used to this…to this body-and-soul event.

She wrapped her arms around his neck, brushed her lips over his ear.

"I was afraid."

His head jerked back and that onyx gaze burned into her like fire.

"Afraid of what, Athe—"

She pressed her hand to his mouth, and his jagged, hot breath bathed her palm. The fire in his eyes blazed hotter, but she closed her own and sank her teeth into her bottom lip, choking back a whimper. That only served to emphasize the sensation of him filling her to damn near overflowing, reclaiming her, rebranding her.

"That's why I left you. I was scared of falling so deep in love with you that I'd disappear. That there would be nothing left of me. I was terrified of loving you more than myself. Of what I'd do because of it."

Like stay with a man whose heart was so hardened, he couldn't love her back.

Shivering, she rose off his cock, pleasure rippling through her as his thick, hard flesh dragged over her slick, sensitive core. When only the tip of him nudged her entrance, she plunged back down, driving the air from her lungs and a small scream from her throat. Panting, she kissed his ear, the rim of it, the lobe.

"Not a day hasn't gone by that I didn't second-guess my decision," she rasped, voice hoarse. "Because, no, you aren't perfect. But you're beautiful, protective, loyal. You're imperfect perfection, and I—"

He yanked her hand from his mouth and slammed his lips to hers, swallowing whatever else she would've confessed. Thank God. Because with her sex full of him and too many emotions shoving against her chest, she might have said something she couldn't have taken back. Something that would've left her more naked, spread open and exposed then she was right now in the back of this limousine.

"Ride me, dammit," he demanded in a ragged, hoarse voice.

And she obeyed.

She rode him with uninhibited abandon, rising and falling, grinding into him, fucking him. His growled praise urged her to take him, and with every raw compliment, each hoarse command, he shoved her closer and closer to release. Electricity sizzled through her, and she opened her arms to it, transforming into pleasure's willing conduit. And when he reached between them and rubbed the nub of engorged flesh, she soared.

In the grip of her orgasm, he followed, thrusting and pouring into her. She held him through it, relishing the evidence of his desire for her. Of their cataclysmic desire for each other. With his raw shout still ringing in her ears, she buried her face in his neck, clinging to him.

A quiet settled around them, and only then did she realize that the limo had stopped. Damn, how long had they been sitting... Where? She lifted her head high enough to glance at the smoked-out window and glimpsed the front of her condominium's building.

Leaning forward, Nico pressed a button under the divider.

"Please take us to my penthouse."

"Yes, sir," came his driver's clear, disembodied voice.

"That okay with you?" Nico asked, hitting the button again and glancing down at her. "I don't want to be done tonight."

"Yes, it's okay."

He threaded his fingers through her hair, smoothing the curls away from her face.

"Good," he murmured.

She should be at least a little embarrassed that the driver must know they'd been fucking. But for the life of her, curled up against Nico, breathing in his sandalwood-and-sex scent, still full and throbbing from the delicious burn of his fierce possession, she couldn't bring herself to care.

And as the limousine pulled away from the curb and headed toward his penthouse, she closed her eyes and brushed her lips against the base of his throat, savoring the beat of his pulse against her lips.

Tomorrow.

Tomorrow would be soon enough to worry about the actions and consequences of tonight. Because she didn't fool herself. There would be consequences. But…

Tomorrow.

Eleven

The scent of vanilla, sugar and sex greeted Nico before he opened his eyes, and he burrowed his face into the source of it. Immediately, images from the previous evening and early morning hours flooded him.

The best fucking limousine ride of his life.

He and Athena back at his high-rise penthouse, in his bedroom, losing themselves in each other time and time again. Him taking her like a man possessed.

Like a man unsure of when he'd touch her, taste her again.

Yeah, he'd been frenzied.

And now his bed and the tangled sheet were empty.

He didn't need to open his eyes or stretch out his hand to touch the cool sheet to verify that. An emptiness in the room and in his chest did it.

Sitting up, he scanned the room, confirming what he'd known. Athena had slipped out.

Disappointment burrowed deep within him. He tried to deny it, but shit, what was the point? He tossed a look at the digital clock on his nightstand. Six ten. How long had she been gone? Did she wait for the fucking sweat to dry—

"Hey, you're awake." She stood in the open bedroom door, his white dress shirt draped around her. And it had never looked that good on him. "Hi."

"Hey." More than that one word piled up in his throat, but none of them emerged. He could only stare at those gorgeous curls piled on top of her head, at those long, slender brown legs bared under his shirt's hem. At that lovely face wearing a shy yet beautiful smile. "What're you doing up?"

She arched an eyebrow, her gaze dipping to his dick that tented the sheet over his hips. Hell, she made him hard. Why deny that either? Especially when just last night he'd admitted to being celibate for three years.

"I planned on making breakfast for us and went to your kitchen to see what you had. Which, to answer that? Everything. I was thinking an omelet, bacon and French toast? Sounds good?"

"Sounds perfect. After I have you." He stretched out a hand toward her and watched with satisfaction as her chest quickly rose and fell and her hazel eyes brightened with lust. "Come here, baby girl."

She took a step toward him, then her cell phone rang; he recognized her ring tone from last night.

His arm dropped and dread curled in his gut as did a

sense of déjà vu. He'd been here before with her. Three years ago.

Athena glanced toward the phone she'd left on the nightstand sometime last night, frowning.

"Go on." He hiked a chin in its direction. "Answer it."

They both knew she would, just as they both knew who it was on the other end of the call.

Indecision warred on her face, but Nico settled the battle by throwing back the sheet and swinging his legs over the end of the bed. He stood and crossed to the bathroom, closing the door behind him.

By the time he showered, brushed his teeth and emerged with a towel wrapped around his hips, Athena sat on the edge of the mattress, dressed in the red gown from the previous evening. A helpless anger burned inside him, and he strode to his walk-in closet, grabbing a pair of sweatpants and jerking them on. He used several more minutes to calm his temper before reentering his bedroom. But the helplessness clung to him like a burr he couldn't shake.

He hated it.

Resented her for its return.

"I take it this means breakfast is off," he said, crossing his arms over his chest.

"Nico, I'm sorry." She rose, spreading her hands in front of her, palms up. "That was Mom."

"Of course it was." He nodded. "Let me guess. She needs you at home. Or no, wait. There's a problem at the bakery."

Her wince supplied his answer.

"I'm sorry," she repeated, her arms falling to her

sides. "Randall's a no-show at the bakery, Kira's sick and another employee called in. She's shorthanded. Plus, she hasn't worked in the store for a long time. She's not familiar with how it runs. She needs me, and I can't…" She shook her head, her shoulders lifting and falling in a shrug. "I can't just leave her hanging."

"Of course you can't."

Athena sighed, pinching the bridge of her nose. "Nico, don't do this. Not after… Please, just try and understand."

"Not after what? Not after last night?" The temper he'd tried to rein in snapped at its tethers. "What does last night have to do with this?" He waved a hand between them. "I'm having a wicked fucking case of déjà vu, Athena. But the difference between then and now? I refuse to beg you to stand up for yourself. To set boundaries for yourself, for us. Because there is no us. So no, I don't have to understand. This is you. This is who you insist on being. I can't fight to make you see different, to be different when you don't want that for yourself."

"What do you want me to do, dammit?" she snapped. "Throw my mother to the wolves? Tell her, 'Sorry you're in a tough spot, sucks to be you'? Yes, they can be annoying and trying as hell, but they're still family. I can't abandon them."

"Did I ever once ask you to do that, Athena?" he growled, advancing a step on her.

He drew to a halt, whipping around and stalking in the opposite direction. Thrusting his fingers through his hair, he fisted the strands, the bite of pain centering him before he faced her again.

"I never asked you to give up your family for me,

Athena. I never tried to isolate you as they accused me of doing. I only asked that you make room for me, for us. Which meant setting boundaries, protecting our relationship. So if we were in the middle of lunch and your brother called, saying your mother needed you home to help cook for that evening's dinner, you didn't drop everything, including me, to go do their bidding. Or if your grandmother ordered you to leave the bakery so Randall could man a shift and learn responsibility, you still chose to stay 'just in case.' But that meant showing up an hour late to our evening together. Or calling at all hours for whatever reason even though it didn't just disturb you but your man. If you didn't make our relationship a priority or respect it, why would your family?" He dropped his arms to his sides and twisted his mouth into a humorless smile. "You're an enabler, Athena. They will never find out if they can manage their own lives or that bakery because you won't step back, take your hands off and let them. And you won't, because you're afraid they'll discover they don't need you."

"That's not true," she whispered, flinching.

Stop, a voice demanded. *Stop this now.*

But he couldn't. And he didn't.

"Yeah, it is. You're terrified they won't depend on you, and then what would your place be in the Evans family? Where would you belong? Would they love you less? It scares the shit out of you to find out the answers to those questions."

"Stop it." She threw her hands up, as if warding off him and his words. *"Stop, Nico."*

The pain in her voice shut him up as effectively as a hand being clapped over his mouth.

Their rough breaths punctuated the air, and his harsh words seemed to echo in the room. That same voice that urged him to stop also pushed him to apologize, but he couldn't. The delivery might have sucked, but he'd spoken the truth.

Still… His palms itched to hold her, soothe her.

"I'm going to leave," she said, her hazel eyes dark, haunted.

And he'd done that.

"I'll call my driver to take you home." He moved toward his phone, because as much as she wanted to leave, he also needed her to go.

This… It fucked with his head. Took him back to a place he'd vowed never to return. A place where he'd been vulnerable, weak, her puppet.

Love's victim.

"You don't need to do that. I can call—"

"Athena, my driver picked you up, he'll take you home," Nico ground out.

She shrugged. "Fine. I just… Fine."

Turning, she walked out of his bedroom.

And he didn't follow.

Déjà vu, indeed.

"Whew, either I'm getting old, or I completely forgot how busy this place can get. Probably a little of both." Winnie chuckled, dropping into the chair behind the desk in the office.

"And we still have the afternoon rush to go," Athena warned with a smile, sinking into the visitor's chair with a sigh. "All those hungry college students pouring in after evening classes and people needing a snack on their way home from work."

Winnie groaned, covering her eyes with her arm. "Well thank goodness for them," she said with another laugh. "They're how we keep the lights on." She dropped her arm, smiling, a wistful note in her voice. "I have no idea how your grandmother did it all those years and never seemed tired. Not one day. Like you. Honey, thank you for coming in today. As soon as you showed up, a calm settled over me. I didn't have to worry about a thing. And neither did the staff. Everything just flowed so smoothly. Thank you."

"You're welcome."

She should leave it there, with her mother's gratitude spreading through her like liquid sunshine. But she couldn't.

You're afraid they'll discover they're capable and don't need you... You're terrified they won't depend on you and then what would your place be in the Evans family? Would they love you less? It scares the shit out of you to find out the answers...

All morning and afternoon, Nico's words haunted her. No, that wasn't accurate. The truth in them haunted her.

He was right. Not just about how she hadn't placed boundaries with her family, but that she enabled them. And she did it for herself, not them. She did it out of fear, out of a need to belong. A need to be an Evans. But the time had come to stop hiding. From the truth, and from herself.

"Mom?"

"Yes, honey?"

"Why didn't you call Randall to come in and help you today?" She inhaled. *Do it. Just...do it.* "Actually, why isn't Randall here instead of you? Especially since his presence at the bakery was part of our deal."

Irritation crossed her mother's expression before she flattened her hands on the desk.

"Athena, not this again." Winnie shrugged a shoulder. "Your brother is involved in a new business deal. A new chain of barbershops. He had something come up so I volunteered to come in. It's no big deal."

"And the last time I had to step in and take care of payroll?" she countered. "Where was he then?"

"Athena," her mother snapped. "Stop this. I'm getting tired of your constant criticisms of Randall. And don't think I don't know where this is coming from."

"Oh really? That's news to me. The constant criticisms and the source. Care to enlighten me?"

Blowing out a breath, her mother flicked a hand. "Please, Athena. Your brother told me how he called you to come over the other night but you were too busy with Nico. You're putting *that man* before family again. And you remember how that turned out last time."

"*That man* is helping us save the bakery, remember? The bakery Randall placed in jeopardy in the first place. Have you asked him about the loan, or did you just ignore that like you did asking him to take on his responsibility at the store?"

Anger flashed in her mother's brown eyes and she straightened in her chair.

"Excuse me? I don't know where this disrespect is coming from, but I'm still your mother, and you won't talk to me like that," she demanded. "I didn't realize it was such a hardship for you to help us out."

Athena jerked, her hands clutching the arms of her chair. A disbelieving laugh tumbled out of her.

"Are you seriously saying that to me? *Me?*" She pressed a hand between her breasts. "I sacrifice everything for this family. Right now, I'm repaying the loan for Randall. You didn't even expect him to do it. It became my responsibility, and I did it. Because I've always done everything I could for all of us, including cleaning up Randall's messes. Who has run this bakery every day since Mama's stroke? Me. Even when you and Dad turned the store over to Randall, I continued to come here every day and run this place because *he doesn't care.* He can't be bothered to be accountable because no one—not you, Dad or me—has demanded it of him."

"Is that what this is about?" Winnie tilted her head, studying Athena. "Your father and I signing the bakery over to Randall instead of you? I understand you worked here with Mama and were very close with her, but you have to know why we made that decision. He's the oldest. It's only right that he should—"

A blast of cold swept through her.

The import of her mother's words must've hit her seconds after she uttered the words. Winnie's face fell, her fingers fluttering to her parted lips. "Oh, honey, I didn't... You know what I meant..."

But Athena had already risen to her feet. She moved as if through a fog.

He's the oldest. It's only right... He's the oldest. It's only right...

The incriminating statement continued to hit her like punches to the chest. Each strike ripped back the curtain on her secret fear, confirming it. Yes, she believed her mother slipped, but that didn't make the sentiment any less true.

Her parents saw Randall as the oldest Evans child. Because he was blood.

And Athena…wasn't.

"Athena! Wait, don't go—"

But she walked out, closing the office door behind her. Somehow she made it through the bakery, answering those who called out to her, putting one foot in front of the other, pushing out the front door.

The warm late afternoon air couldn't breach the ice encasing her. By rote, she reached into the back pocket of her jeans and pulled her cell free. There was only one person she could call, and without conscious thought, she pulled up his contact and dialed.

And when his voice resounded in her ear, the first crack snaked across the numb shield she'd wrapped herself in.

"Nico," she rasped. "I need you."

Twelve

For the second time that day, Nico woke up to an empty bed.

But unlike earlier this morning, he didn't wonder about Athena's whereabouts.

The scents emanating from the kitchen and into his bedroom assured him he could find her there. Climbing off the bed, he stretched, his attention catching on the clock. Eight twenty-five. About six hours since he'd broken several traffic rules speeding over to Brighton after that phone call from Athena.

Nico, I need you.

If he dwelled too long on it, he could still taste the faint residue of terror on his tongue. That drive from his office to the bakery had been the shortest and longest of his life. He'd pulled up outside of the store, spotted her standing on the curb, arms wrapped tightly around herself. He'd started to calm—until she'd lifted her head and he'd glimpsed those haunted hazel eyes. The fierce, howling need to destroy whatever had placed the pain in those golden depths roared inside him like an animal.

She'd whispered, "You were right," and fell into his arms, sobbing as if someone had died—or broken her heart.

He'd guided her into his car and taken her home.

Not the downtown penthouse.

But his home. The one he'd bought a couple of years ago that she'd never been to. She'd seemed to barely notice the drive to Beacon Hill much less the classic, Greek revival home as he lifted her from the car, into the house and up the sweeping staircase to the second level. As soon as he'd laid her on the bed in the master suite, she'd passed out, either from the crying or exhaustion. Maybe both. After removing her shoes and stripping off his jacket, tie and shoes, he'd crawled behind her and curled his body around hers. And they'd slept.

But now, as he made his way down the stairs to the kitchen, he needed answers. First being, was she okay? Second, what had he been right about?

He moved into the kitchen and the sweet scents of caramel, sugar and cream greeted him. It didn't take him long to locate Athena at the wide marble island, a tiny frown of concentration creasing her brow as she slid cookies from a pan to a plate.

"Well, you've been busy," he said, leaning a hip against the counter and crossing his arms.

She didn't jump, but continued moving the cookies and waved toward the cake next to them.

"Snickerdoodle cookies and raspberry sponge cake

with caramel crunch and crème brûlée topping." She briefly peeked up at him with a wary smile. "I hope you don't mind. I bake when I can't sleep."

"You could've woken me up."

She shook her head once. "This is a beautiful house. A gorgeous kitchen."

"Thank you." He pushed off the counter and stepped closer, stopping on the other side of the island. "Let's get it out of the way. Nine bedrooms, eight baths. I bought it two years ago with the thought of having a place to entertain, but I haven't yet. I have two formal dining rooms, one with a domed skylight, a living room, family room, library, a two-story balcony and a walled garden and patio. I'll give you the full tour later. For now, tell me what you meant by saying I was right. What happened to have you crying in my arms?"

She finished with the cookies and flattened her palms on the marble island top.

"Like I said, you were right. About my family. About me. I was scared of those answers. And for good reason. They were what I feared—all along."

"Baby," he murmured.

"No." She shot up a hand and stepped back. "You were right. All these years I've been working, sacrificing, giving everything to them and to the store. No complaining. Ever. Because that's what family does. But they never saw me as family. Or real family. Not where it counts. I'm not a real Evans. And all these years I've tried to earn their love, earn my place, when I can't. I'll never be enough for them. I'll never be an Evans."

"Athena." He rounded the island and took her into his arms. Her fists curled into the front of his shirt, and she buried her face in his chest. She didn't cry, but her frame shook against him. "Athena."

Gripping her hips, he lifted her onto the island. Moving in between her thighs, he pinched her chin and tipped her head up. The brown in her eyes nearly swallowed the green and gold, and he smoothed the pad of his thumb over her cheekbone.

"Do I have complaints about your family? Yes. But have I ever doubted their love for you? Never. That's evident in how they look at you, talk about you. Maybe they don't always treat you with fairness—and no, they don't—yet it's not out of maliciousness but ignorance. Baby girl, my questions were less about them and more about you. About you discovering who you were outside of them. You are more than Winnie Evans's daughter or Randall's big sister. You're even more than Glory Evans's granddaughter. What is your place in this world? If it's not the bakery, why are you not out there claiming it? You deserve so much more than what you're settling for. And you're settling out of fear of rejection. That's not fair to them and it's damn sure not fair to you. That's what I wanted you to think about."

"Who would I be without the bakery?" she said, the note of uncertainty in her voice reaching into his chest and fisting his heart. "For so long, it's been the center of my world. It's where I learned about baking and fell in love with it. It's where Mama became my best friend, not just my grandmother." She settled her palm on his chest, over his heart. "You've thought all this time that I agreed to your bargain to save Randall. That's not true. I did it because of my grandmother. She built Evans Bakery, her and my grandfather. She put everything of herself into it. I couldn't see it sold off as collateral because of Randall's selfishness and greed. Not her legacy. It was only for her."

He should've guessed. Hell, Athena had moved residences for Glory. The truth leaped to his tongue. If he had a soul, a conscience, he'd tell her right now that he'd paid off that loan weeks ago. But he didn't. Because if she knew, he couldn't be certain she'd stay the remaining two months. And he hadn't accomplished his goal yet.

Yes, keep telling yourself that's the reason you want her here.

He briefly closed his eyes. It *had* to be about the business deal, nothing else. He couldn't let it be about anything else. Because now or two months from now, Athena would walk. It was what she did.

"Athena, your grandmother never intended the bakery to become your burden. Her legacy is here—" he gently tapped her temple "—and here." He brushed his fingers over her breast, her heart. "It's the reason she called me and asked for help. She knew you wouldn't reach for your own freedom, so she sought to give it to you. That's how much she wanted you to be free, to be happy. To be fulfilled. Baby, *you* are Glory's legacy, not the building."

She closed her eyes and bowed her head. He didn't disturb her, and moments later, when she grazed her lips over his, he let her take whatever she needed from him.

"Thank you." She pressed a kiss to the corner of his mouth. "Thank you for that."

"You're welcome."

She tunneled her fingers through his hair and drew

him down to her. He met her halfway, and as her tongue thrust between his lips, he met her there, too. He allowed her to take the lead, set the pace. But all those good intentions burned to ashes when she trailed a hand down his chest, abdomen and cupped his cock through his pants.

"Baby girl…" He growled a warning, covering her hand with his.

"I want to lose myself in you, Nico. Please let me."

Not lose herself in pleasure, but in him. No way in hell he could resist that plea.

He took control of the kiss, bending her head back as he unleashed his hunger on her. Cupping her jaw, he tilted her head and dived deep, taking, consuming, gorging on her. And Athena devoured him right back.

"Move that," he ordered, nodding to the desserts behind her.

She quickly obeyed, sliding the dishes to the side, and he balled up the hem of her shirt in his fists and jerked the top over her head. After tossing it to the floor, he stripped off her jeans and panties, leaving her naked on the island. The most delicious meal that would ever be eaten out of this kitchen.

And fuck, did he eat.

Bending, he hauled her legs over his shoulders and spread her wide for his gaze and his fingers. And his mouth. He touched, licked and sucked every part of her. He pumped his fingers into her fluttering entrance. Licked a greedy path up her folds. Sucked on the engorged bundle of nerves at the top of her beautiful sex, loving every shudder that denoted her climbing pleasure. She wanted to lose herself in him? No, he could lose himself in her. Right here.

Above him, her cries caressed his ears. Her hips writhed, twisted, and he crossed an arm low on her belly to hold her in place. He corkscrewed his wrist, finger fucking her and searching out that smooth patch of skin high inside her. Rubbing it, he suckled her clit, granting her no mercy, and from her demands not to stop, it didn't appear Athena wanted any.

In seconds, she stiffened under his mouth, her sex clamping down on his fingers. Her scream rebounded off the walls of the kitchen. And while his dick furiously pounded, he still thrust his fingers, giving her every measure of the orgasm rocking through her. Only when she slumped back on the island, did he lift his head. And attack his zipper.

Goddamn, he needed inside her. Now.

"Athena?" He placed a hot, open-mouthed kiss below her navel. "Yes or no?"

"Yes. Please, yes." She reached for him, her dark curls wild around her face and shoulders. Her eyes glazed with pleasure and mouth swollen from his. "Inside me."

Before she finished the demand, he seated his cock deep inside her. Her gasp bathed his chest, and he tangled a hand in her hair, pulling her head back so he could taste that gasp for himself. Tugging her to the very edge of the island, he withdrew from her, the drag of her tight, hot sex over his hard, thick flesh hauling a soul-deep groan from him. Mimicking the thrust of his tongue, he pushed back in.

Holy…

Nothing like it. Nothing in the world.

Her whimpers spilled into his mouth, and he took every one of them even as he pistoned into her, over and over. The slap of bodies and the sweet suction of her sex accepting and releasing him punctuated the room. She took him so perfectly, as if she was created just for him.

"Touch yourself, baby girl," he rumbled against her lips. "Take us both there."

Eagerly, she reached between their straining bodies and swirled her fingers over the top of her sex, circling, getting there, getting there...

With a loud cry, she went rigid and detonated in his arms.

That beautiful core seized him, milking him, demanding he follow her over the edge, and after three, four more thrusts into her spasming channel, he did.

And for once, he didn't worry about where he landed.

Thirteen

Nico glanced down at his watch, noting the time, then frowned toward his study door. He had a meeting at the office in an hour and a half. If he didn't, he would have done the unthinkable and called in today. Or at the very least, worked from home.

He'd left Athena sleeping in his bed. The corner of his mouth lifted. For once.

As soon as the thought passed through his head, he frowned at the jolt of warmth that thought brought. Oh shit. What was he doing?

He didn't fucking know anymore.

"Mr. Morgan." His housekeeper appeared in the doorway of his study. "There's a gentleman at the door to see you."

Surprised, Nico blinked. In the two years he'd been

in this house, he'd never had a visitor. And who in the hell would arrive at seven thirty in the morning?

"Who is it?" he asked Phillip.

"He says his name is—"

"It's me, Achilles." Achilles Farrell filled the doorway behind Phillip, dwarfing the other man. "Sorry, patience has never been my strong suit. Neither have manners."

Nico should've been annoyed—hell, the man walked into his house without an invitation—but instead, he had to smother a snort. From what he'd come to know about Achilles, he wasn't lying.

"Phillip, it's fine. Thank you."

The housekeeper nodded, stepped aside so Achilles could enter and closed the door behind him.

"Well, I would be lying if I said this isn't a surprise," Nico said, rounding the desk and crossing the room, his arm outstretched. "What brings you by, Achilles?"

"Good news that I wanted to deliver in person." He clasped Nico's hand and squeezed it before reaching into the back pocket of his jeans and removing a thin cigar. As Nico accepted the gift, Achilles grinned, and holy shit. This was the first time Nico had ever seen him fully smile. Joy lit up his blue-gray eyes and handsome face like the sun. "I'm a dad."

Happiness for Achilles bloomed inside Nico's chest. The man's pride and his absolute love for his wife and child beamed from him. Underneath the happiness, though, threaded sadness and confusion. Sadness because he could only congratulate Achilles as a business associate and not as a brother. And confusion, because why was Achilles here, in Nico's home, at this early hour telling him news that should be shared with family?

"Congratulations, Achilles." Nico smiled, clapping him on the shoulder. "To you and Mycah. I'm happy for both of you."

"Thank you." Achilles nodded toward the cigar. "Natia Michelle Farrell was born yesterday morning. Nine pounds, eight ounces. I just left the hospital this morning to go home and get some things for Mycah, to shower and change clothes. I pretty much hate all this fancy society bullshit, but I've always wanted to give out cigars if I ever had a kid. Since Cain and Kenan were already at the hospital, I gave them theirs. But I couldn't go without giving my last cigar to my other brother on my little girl's birth."

"Thank—" Shock rippled through Nico, an icy avalanche that smothered him. "I'm sorry—what?" he rasped.

Achilles nodded again, his Farrell eyes too piercing. "My brother. Yeah, I know. Your eyes may be different than Cain's, Kenan's and mine, but I don't think you realize how much you and Cain resemble each other. The resemblance plus you buying up Farrell stock under different names and companies. The damnedest things happen when they put the bored IT guy in the basement. He digs. And when you started being nice—" he growled the word as if it were a curse "—and bringing your fiancée around, well, that kicked off all my spidey senses. Didn't take long to dig up birth certificates and old history. Barron thought he was a slick motherfucker, but he wasn't. And he had a hidden file on you inches thick. Metaphorically speaking, anyway. He didn't like you very much. Which might put you in the running for my favorite brother."

Nico couldn't speak. Not when shock still gripped him. *He knew.* Achilles knew they were brothers. Relief, joy, fear and sorrow crashed into him, nearly knocking him to his ass. He locked his knees against the wave of emotions.

"The questions is," Achilles continued, eyes narrowing on Nico, "what are your plans now? I'll be the first to admit, I'm not a natural businessman. But I have common sense and I know enough to recognize a hostile takeover when I see one. You plan to take over Farrell International and from there, I can't guess. But I won't let you. Not because of the money or the power. Fuck that. I didn't have it months ago—I can provide for my family if all this shit goes away tomorrow. Hell—" a smile flickered over his mouth "—my wife could take care of us. But I won't let you for Cain and Kenan. I haven't told them about you yet, but I plan to. I just wanted to talk to you first and judge for myself that you're the man I believe you to be."

"Is that why you're here? To warn me?" Nico asked, his heart pounding.

He couldn't think. Or rather, too many thoughts whirled in his head. Part of him longed to grab his brother—now that he could call him that aloud—and sit down, talk with him, laugh with him…as brothers. As family. Something he yearned for, especially with his mother gone.

But the other part of him, the part that'd had every outstretched hand slapped away and every trust betrayed, couldn't believe in this. That part curled up on itself, afraid to…hope. That part would rather be suspicious and harbor no expectations that could be hurled to the ground.

"Is that what you heard from all of that? So like Cain," Achilles muttered. "I'm telling you the same thing our brother once told me. You're not alone. Not anymore. You're our brother, one of us. And we'll fight for you. Even if we have to fight against you while we're doing it. That's all right. What brothers don't brawl? But get that through your head. *We'll fight for you.* All you have to do is stop being so goddamn stubborn. Now, don't wait too long. I'll show back up here, and I won't be alone." Dipping his chin at the cigar. "Enjoy it."

Then Achilles strode out of the study, leaving emotional chaos in his wake.

"Did that just happen?"

He jerked his head up, and Athena appeared in the doorway. Once more, she wore one of his dress shirts, and she stared at him, hazel eyes wide, full lips parted.

"Did Achilles Farrell just out you?"

Hell.

Athena moved into the study, giving the cavernous room with its dark wood furniture, expensive rugs and floor-to-ceiling bookshelves a cursory scan. All of her focus remained on Nico, who stood in the center of the room like a statue. If it'd been anyone else, she might've called it shell shock. But it wasn't anyone else. And even as she watched, those obsidian eyes sharpened and Nico thrust his fingers through his hair, tugging the waves away from his face. Wheeling on his heel, he stalked across the room to the large bay window, staring out of it to the garden below.

"Nico?" She followed him, settling a hand on the center of his back. "I didn't mean to eavesdrop but when I heard voices…"

"You eavesdropped."

"I did." There wasn't any point in denying it. "But it sounded like Achilles wasn't mad. At all. Actually, that last part sounded like he wanted to welcome you as his brother. He believed Cain and Kenan would, too."

"So he said."

She frowned at the flat tone, and it took everything in her not to grab him by the arms and shake him. Get some kind of reaction.

"This is good, right?" She tried again, leaning forward to peer at his strong, chiseled profile. That's what he reminded her of now. A man fashioned from stone. "You can go to them, be honest. Be brothers. Be a family. Give up on this silly revenge plan."

"Silly revenge plan?" He finally turned, an eyebrow arched high. "Justice for the way that man threw my mother away, threw me away is silly? Justice for every menial job, every shitty apartment, every asshole boss and pitiful check just to put food on the table, clothes on my back and a roof over my head? That's silly? Justice for her dying too fucking early is silly?" he growled. "What does Achilles Farrell showing up here change about any of that?"

"Nothing can change the past. Not even God can do that. All we have is the present and hope we're writing our future. And you have the opportunity to do that, Nico. Write a beautiful future that is so different from your past. But you can't if you're determined to hang on to it."

He snorted, walking away from her to his desk.

"That sounds pretty, Athena. But that has nothing to do with real life. I made a promise to my mother, to myself, that I would make Barron Farrell pay, and I'm not going back on it. Not for anyone. Or anything."

"I was at Rhoda's funeral." His shoulders stiffened, but he didn't turn and look at her, didn't speak. Didn't react at all to the news that she'd attended his mother's homegoing service. "Even though we were no longer together, I had to pay my respects to the woman who welcomed me into your small family like a daughter. The woman I knew wouldn't have approved of this path you're going down. And not out of concern for Barron. But because she loved you so much. She would've known that revenge, spite, hate—they don't just leave their mark on the intended victim. They leave scars on you. And she would've hated that for you."

"You don't know what you're talking about," he snapped, spinning around, eyes flashing. And in that moment, as she glimpsed the anger, the pain, the hurt in that gaze, she knew… She *knew*.

She'd lost him.

"I do," she softly countered. "But you're so stuck in your hate that you can't see past it." She shook her head, spreading her hands, fingers splayed wide. "Remember when you told me how you were filled with hate? For everyone. Barron. Me. Your brothers. Even your mother. But you forgot someone on that list. You. You hate yourself. For not protecting your mother. For not keeping your father in your life. For not saving your mother in time. For not being worthy. For all manner of bullshit reasons. And make no mistake—they're bullshit reasons.

But that doesn't make them any less real for you. And because you can't love yourself, you'll never be able to accept the love of anyone else. Not your brothers. Not me," she murmured.

Confessed.

Because she did love him. Had possibly never stopped.

And that made her an idiot. Especially since he still didn't return the affection.

She closed her eyes, drew in a deep, shaky breath that hurt.

"I'm out," she quietly said.

His eyes narrowed, and he slid his hands into the front pockets of his suit pants. But she didn't miss the tension that entered his body.

"You're out," he softly repeated. "We have a bargain."

"Yes. And I'm breaking it."

"You're running," he accused, his mouth twisting into a grim smile. "You're running back to your family." He let loose a harsh laugh. "Your brother told me this would happen. Warned me he could follow through on his threat again. And he did, didn't he?"

"What're you talking about?"

"Ask him about three years ago when he showed up at my house, asking for money. And his threat when I turned him down. He warned me he could get you to walk away from me if I didn't give him what he wanted, even though he knew I intended to propose to you. And he did. Not a week later, you were gone. And last week, he paid me a visit and did the same thing. And here we are. You walking away. Again."

Propose?

Pain bloomed inside her chest, exploding like shattered glass.

"God, you're desperate." Fury at Randall and Nico replaced the hurt, stirring bright inside her. Her fists curled at her thighs, but then the flame extinguished, just leaving her exhausted. And broken. "I feel so sorry for you, Nico. You must be fucking terrified right now if you lobbed that bomb out there between us. Just so you know? I'm not running. If the bank calls the note, they call it. Randall will just have to face the consequences. I'm through cleaning up his mess. I'm also through watching you self-destruct."

She pivoted on her heel and strode across the room but paused at the doorway, holding herself steady by a hand on the jamb. No way in hell would she cry in front of him. She'd wait until she'd gathered her things and was behind her own apartment door for that. It wasn't a lot, but she had her pride.

"So you don't misunderstand what happened here or twist it around to suit your narrative. I didn't leave you. You pushed me out this door. I love you. I love all of you—every brilliant, driven, generous, vulnerable, stubborn, arrogant, broken and beautiful bit of you. You're utterly perfect in my eyes. But I can't stay with someone who's scared of life. Scared to live. Scared to love. I won't remain in a prison with you. When you decide to be as free as you told me I should be, come find me."

Then she walked out.

Probably for good.

And she did it, knowing she would have to be okay with that possibility.

Fourteen

Nico knocked on the door of the mansion that had housed four generations of Farrells. At one time—as recently as a week ago—that thought had angered him. But now it didn't even evoke a flinch. Now he just didn't care.

And hadn't that been his problem for the last five days?

He didn't care.

Not about the meeting he'd scheduled with Mark Hanson that would've given him more Farrell International shares.

Not even about the meeting he headed into right now.

The emptiness that had dropped into his chest when Athena had announced she loved him, then left his home—his life—had only yawned wider, engulfing him.

Why he'd agreed to this particular meeting? Hell,

he couldn't answer that himself. Nothing good could come from it. When Cain Farrell called and asked him to come to his Beacon Hill home instead of the offices at Farrell International, Nico had known something was different. If he'd been the smart businessman his reputation lauded him to be, he'd have shown up with a lawyer. But no, he'd arrived at Cain's to face God knew what and couldn't summon up a single fuck. He was fresh out.

The same butler from before opened the door, and in moments he stood in the doorway of the library. His brothers waited for him.

Cain stood in front of his desk, his hands in his pants pockets while Kenan perched on the desk. Achilles leaned against one of the floor-to-ceiling shelves, arms crossed over his chest. They all stared at him.

"Well, don't just stand there. Come on in here and let's get a look at you," Kenan called.

As if they'd never met. But then again, they never had—not as brothers.

Still suspicious of the almost jovial tone, Nico moved into the library. He stopped several feet in front of them, tension vibrating through him, braced for…anything.

Anything but the hard, fierce embrace that Cain yanked him into.

"He's getting so soft in his dotage," Nico heard Kenan stage-whisper.

Achilles snorted in reply.

But Nico dimly paid attention to this byplay. The man hugging him consumed all of his attention. That and the tight ball of emotion pressing against Nico's sternum. Slowly, Nico lifted his arms and wrapped them around Cain, returning the embrace.

After several moments, Cain pounded him on the back and released him, clearing his throat as he stepped back.

"We don't get some of that?" Kenan grinned, holding his arms wide and hopping off the desk.

Before Nico could agree or object, his younger brother pulled him into a hard, quick embrace, too. And that knot of emotion in Nico's chest expanded.

"I'm not hugging you." Achilles grunted. "I gave you a cigar."

Kenan snickered, and in spite of the shock swirling through him at this strange turn of events, Nico snorted.

"Now," Cain said, pinning him with his straightforward blue-gray stare. "Where the hell have you been? Why didn't you come to us instead of trying to conduct a hostile takeover?"

"Right, Morgan." Kenan tsk-tsked. "Bad form."

Nico waited for his usual defensiveness to rise up within him. Waited for that resentment to take over. But nothing. Nothing but the truth tumbled out of him. And he didn't hold back. He revealed everything about Barron abandoning him and his mother, from his rough childhood, to spying on Cain and his family, to Barron visiting him and then Barron trying to destroy his business. And finally to his mother's death and his decision to get revenge on their dead father by ruining his beloved company.

"I'm sorry about your mother," Cain said. "If anyone understands how much of a bastard Barron was, it's me." Pain spasmed across his face before it hardened.

His head bowed for several seconds before he lifted it again with a stoic expression. "I'll tell you like I told Achilles and Kenan. I grew up with Barron, but I'm not the lucky one—you were. He was a bastard who used his fists to get a point across as much as his voice. So I don't blame you for wanting to go after his company. It was the only fucking thing he loved. It's what I would've done in your position."

"It was brilliant," Achilles said. "If I hadn't gone looking for something on you, I wouldn't have caught it. But why didn't you come to us? Why the charade with Athena? Are you two even engaged?"

"Because I…" The pat answer of "I didn't trust you," died on his lips. It was past time for honesty. And hadn't that been what Athena had begged of him? To be open? To—how had she put it?—not be scared to live? To love? That included embracing the love of brothers. "Because I wanted this—" he waved a hand between them "—too badly, and I believed I could never have it. Barron didn't want me, why would you?"

"Because Barron was an asshole?" Kenan supplied.

"Yes, there's that." Nico huffed out a short laugh. "But I…couldn't accept it would be that easy."

"And Athena?" Achilles pressed.

"She's real," Nico said. "Well, almost," he amended, then quickly explained their bargain and how he'd fucked up their relationship.

"Oh yeah." Achilles grunted. "You're a Farrell. Fucking shit up with your woman. That's another trait."

Kenan winced. "Ouch. True. What're you going to do about that?"

Nico shook his head. "I don't know." He glanced

at the men in front of him, and for the first time, he found himself with a support system. One that didn't judge him. One that, with time, might one day…love him. One he could love in return. That possibility alone whispered at him to take a chance. To risk it. "I love her," he murmured.

God, he loved her.

And he was tired of being scared.

Of running.

He'd accused her of running, but it'd been him all this time.

Kenan rolled his eyes. "Of course you do." He clapped his hands in glee. "Fortunately for you, I am the relationship whisperer in this crew. I single-handedly saved both of their asses."

"Revisionist history," Cain drawled.

"Anyway," Kenan said loudly, "we got your back."

"Hold on, Millionaire Matchmaker." Cain held up his hands and turned to Nico, his smirk falling from his lips. "Nico, I asked you here for one more thing. Kenan, Achilles and I talked this over. Barron might not have recognized you, but we do. You're the oldest, and if things had been fair, you would've been CEO of Farrell. Barron cost you your birthright, your name and tried to destroy your business. And in the end he was responsible for your mother's hard life, which led to her undiagnosed illness. Barron didn't do right by you, but we will. So I'll step aside as CEO for you. We've all agreed on it."

Nico blinked, shock punching through his system. He stared at these men, his brothers, lost for words. And humbled. They would sacrifice for him. They would declare to the world in no louder fashion that he not only belonged to Farrell, but to them.

He squeezed his eyes closed against the sudden sting.

"Oh shit. We broke him," Kenan whispered.

Yeah, they did.

They absolutely did.

Fifteen

"Well this is a little dramatic, isn't it?" Randall strode into the bakery office, grinning. "Hey, Mom."

Athena didn't answer her brother as he approached their mother, swooping her into an embrace and planting a kiss on her cheek. Usually, Winnie would glow under Randall's charm and attention—he had that effect on people, didn't matter age or sex—but today, she patted his shoulder and murmured a subdued greeting.

It'd been a week since their conversation in this office, and while Winnie had tried to call Athena, she hadn't been in the space to talk to her mother just yet.

Now she was there.

Now she could talk to her from a place of strength.

"Hey, sis." Randall came over to her, sliding an arm around her shoulders and squeezing. "Long time, no see." Dropping a kiss on the top of her head, he rounded the desk and plopped down into the chair. "You called me down here, so what's going on? I didn't know Mom was going to be here, too, though. So much mystery."

God, he was such a chatterbox. Why hadn't it annoyed her before? Oh wait. It had. She'd just sucked it up.

Not any longer.

"Thank you two for coming down here. I'm sorry if it seems a little melodramatic, but I didn't want to do this at home since Dad isn't aware of the situation with the loan." She picked up a folder off the edge of the desk. Opening it, she removed a copy of the note stamped Paid and laid it in front of Randall. "Here's the note for the three-hundred-thousand-dollar loan."

The original had shown up in her mail days ago, and she'd cried. Nico had saved her grandmother's bakery despite Athena not holding up her end of the bargain. Yes, he'd broken her heart, but he'd rescued it, too.

And now, here she stood in front of her brother, giving it away.

The smile evaporated from Randall's face and her mother's soft gasp echoed in the office.

"You did it, Athena," he breathed. "You paid it off. How— I can't believe it." He snatched the document up, gaping at it before lifting his gaze to her. "I don't care how you did it! Thank you!"

"That's the problem," she said, wistfulness creeping into her voice in spite of her best intentions. "You don't care how I did it. Which lets me know you'll jeopardize this bakery again. But it doesn't matter to me anymore. It's no longer my concern because I'm stepping away."

"Athena." Her mother shifted forward, settling a

hand on her arm. "What're you talking about? Is this about what I said—"

"No—yes." Her mother needed to hear the truth. "It is about what you said. And it's also about me. I'm choosing me. While I'm here at this bakery, I'm stuck. I've never given myself a chance to find out who I am outside of it. And I'm excited to find that out. And the fact is, Mom, you and Dad made the decision to give Evans to Randall. So you have to live with that. Good or bad. And so does he. So do you," she said, turning to him. "It's time for you to grow up, Randall. I'm no longer going to be your safety net."

"What're you talking about?" he snapped, rising to his feet, the note clutched in his hand. "You're just going to walk out on us? Leave? This isn't how you treat family!"

"No, what you've been doing for the last few years isn't how you treat family. Mom and Dad won't say it to you, but I will. You're a selfish, spoiled brat. You need to grow up because you have a wife and kids depending on you, and now employees depending on you, too. No one can afford for you to fuck around and find yourself. Oh—" she flattened her palms on the desk and leaned forward, pinning him with an unblinking stare "—if you go to Nico Morgan and try to extort money from him again, I'll disown you without batting an eyelash. And it won't hurt me."

She straightened. And smiled.

"Do better, little brother."

Turning to her mother, she pressed a kiss to her cheek.

"I love you. Please respect me and my decision and

don't call me about this bakery or Randall." Athena hugged her, kissed her again. "I'll call you and keep you updated, okay?"

"Okay, honey," Winnie whispered.

Then, tears stinging her eyes, Athena walked out of the office and the bakery.

And it felt good.

It felt…freeing.

Sixteen

"This is the funniest-looking restaurant I've ever been to," Athena grumbled as she followed Eve through the front entrance of the downtown building that housed Farrell International.

"Hah." Eve smirked over her shoulder. "We're just picking up Devon. She's visiting Cain." She looped her arm through Athena's. "I can't wait to get to Mycah and Achilles's and talk about this new business adventure of yours. A catering company. It makes perfect sense! And I've already told Kenan that Farrell will be your first client."

Athena smiled even as she blinked against the sudden sting of moisture in her eyes at the unconditional show of support from her new friend.

"You didn't have to—"

Eve waved away her soft objection. "Please. That's

what we do. We support one another. And I have it on very good authority that you can cook your ass off."

"Devon," Athena said with a laugh. "Devon is your very good authority."

Eve grinned. "True. And speaking of Devon, where is she? I can't wait to get my hands on little Natia. She's gorgeous, Athena." Eve sighed.

Athena snorted. "You sigh like that again, I'm going to start thinking you're ready for one of your own."

"Bite your tongue, missy." Eve slapped Athena's arm, gasping. "I love babies and want one of my own with Kenan one day. But *one day*. Right now Intimate Curves is the only child I need."

Athena laughed. "And it might keep you up at night sometimes, but at least it doesn't shit in diapers."

"There's that."

Chuckling, Athena scanned the building's lobby. For the first time, she noticed a podium with mics set up at the far end and a throng of people gathered in front of it. An excited hum filled the air.

"I wonder what's going on," she said to Eve.

But Eve didn't answer, as she waved to Devon, who stepped out of the bank of elevators. The petite woman strode toward them, smiling.

"Hey," Devon greeted them. "Let's head over. It's about to start."

"What's about to start?" Athena asked, a seed of suspicion springing roots inside her. She glanced from one woman to the other. "Why do I have the feeling both of you know what's going on and are holding out?"

"Because you're smart as hell," Eve said. "Let's go."

They practically tugged her over to the people

crowded in front of the podium, and before Athena could question them further, Cain, Achilles and Kenan appeared on the platform.

And a moment later, Nico followed.

Oh God.

She stared at him. It'd been over a week since she'd seen him, but it might as well as have been months, years. The punch of hunger, of yearning slammed into her and she sucked in a hard, sharp breath. Dark waves framed his lean, beautiful face, brushing his jaw. And when those onyx eyes swept the throng, she held her breath. Waited... Waited... There. It landed on her, and she lit on fire.

Stop, she wanted to yell at him. *You don't have the right to look at me like that. Like you want me. Like you...love me.*

So she looked away. She switched her gaze to Cain, who stepped up to the bank of mics, but Nico's eyes branded her, and she shivered.

"Thank you for attending this special press conference, especially on such short notice. I'll be brief and won't be accepting questions at this time. We'll set up a separate time for a question and answer session." He glanced behind him at his brothers. "As you know, a year ago, our father, Barron Farrell, died, leaving an unusual stipulation in his will. Achilles Farrell, Kenan Rhodes and myself, who until Barron's death hadn't been aware we were brothers, were directed to manage Farrell International together as siblings for a one-year period. At that time, we were strangers, but we have become true brothers. But our story hasn't ended with just the three of us. We have another brother. Nico

Morgan, who many of you may recognize as the CEO of Brightstar Holdings. He is also the oldest son of Barron Farrell."

The lobby erupted in a cacophony of shouts, questions and camera flashes.

Athena's lips parted, and she jerked her attention away from Cain to Nico. Shock still rippled through her, but so did joy and hope. For him.

"This is the dawn of a new day. We might have started this journey as strangers, but we continue it as brothers. As family. We just adjourned a board meeting. I'm proud to announce that we are now no longer Farrell International. From this day forward, we are Brightstar Farrell Incorporated. We're united by blood and by business. Thank you."

Shouted questions bombarded Cain, but he stepped back from the podium and so did the rest of the Farrell men. Athena couldn't move. Even when Devon and Eve greeted their husband and fiancé, she remained rooted. Even when Nico came to stand before her.

She could only study him, searching for...

"I've missed you."

That.

"I love you."

And that.

"Please forgive me, Athena, for pushing you away. I'm not scared to live, to be. I'm not scared to love you or to be loved by you. Please, baby girl, love me."

And oh God, that.

"Nico," she breathed.

"Because of you, I have a family. But with you, I have a home. I *am* home." He lifted his hands toward her, but at the last second stopped, as if hesitant to touch her. "Let me come home, Athena," he whispered.

Something inside her cracked. Her last resistance. Because she wanted to hold nothing back from him. She decided to give him everything. To risk all of her. Trusting he would never let her fall. He would be there to catch her.

Circling his wrists, she lifted his hands to her cheeks and turned her face into his palm, kissing it.

"I love you," she said. "And I will always run to you. You're where I belong."

With a groan, he kissed her, and she melted into him, opening wide, taking him.

She would always take him. Always welcome him.

Always love him.

* * * * *

Don't miss any of the Billionaires of Boston series
from USA TODAY bestselling author
Naima Simone!

Vows in Name Only
Secrets of a One Night Stand
The Perfect Fake Date
Black Sheep Bargain

#2899 BEST MAN RANCHER
The Carsons of Lone Rock • by Maisey Yates
Widow Shelby Sohappy isn't looking for romance, but there's something enticing about rancher Kit Carson, especially now that they're thrown together for their siblings' wedding. As one night together turns into two, can they let go of their past to embrace a future?

#2900 AN EX TO REMEMBER
Texas Cattleman's Club: Ranchers and Rivals
by Jessica Lemmon
After a fall, Aubrey Collins wakes up with amnesia—and believing her ex, rancher Vic Grandin, is her current boyfriend! The best way to help her? Play along! But when the truth comes to light, their second chance may fall apart...

#2901 HOW TO MARRY A BAD BOY
Dynasties: Tech Tycoons • by Shannon McKenna
To help launch her start-up, Eve Seaton accepts an unbelievable offer from playboy CTO Marcus Moss: his connections for her hand in marriage, which will let him keep his family company. But is this deal too good to be true?

#2902 THE COMEBACK HEIR
by Janice Maynard
Home due to tragedy, exes Felicity Vance and Wynn Oliver don't expect to see one another, but Wynn needs a caregiver for the baby niece now entrusted in his care. But when one hot night changes everything, will secrets from their past ruin it all?

#2903 THE PREGNANCY PROPOSAL
Cress Brothers • by Niobia Bryant
Career-driven Montgomery Morgan and partying playboy chef Sean Cress have one fun night together, no-strings...until they discover she's pregnant. Ever the businesswoman, she proposes a marriage deal to keep up appearances. But no amount of paperwork can hide the undeniable passion between them!

#2904 LAST CHANCE REUNION
Nights at the Mahal • by Sophia Singh Sasson
The investor who fashion designer Nisha Chawla is meeting is...her ex, Sameer Singh. He was her first love before everything went wrong, and now he's representing his family's interests. As things heat up, she must hold on to her heart *and* her business...

SPECIAL EXCERPT FROM

♦ HARLEQUIN

DESIRE

*Recording studio exec Miles Woodson needs a
showstopping act for his charity talent show,
and R&B superstar Cambria Harding fits the bill.
But when long days working together become steamy
nights, can these opposites make both their passion
project and relationship work?*

Read on for a sneak peek at
What Happens After Hours
by Kianna Alexander

"There's no need to insult me, Cambria. After all, we'll
be seeing a lot of each other over the next two weeks."

"Oh, I see. You're the type that can dish it, but can't
take it. Ain't that something?" she scoffed, then shook her
head. "Let's make a deal—I'll show you the same level
of respect you show me." She grabbed her handbag from
the table. "So remember the next time you open your
mouth, you can expect me to match whatever energy you
throw out."

He watched her, silently surveying the way her glossy lips pursed into a straight line, the defiant tilt of her chin, the challenge in her eyes. She was mesmerizing, disconcerting even. No woman had ever affected him this way before. *She knocks me so off balance, but for some reason, I like it.*

Her lips parted. "Why are you staring at me like that?"

Don't miss what happens next in...
What Happens After Hours
by Kianna Alexander.

Available October 2022 wherever
Harlequin Desire books and ebooks are sold.

Harlequin.com